Books By Donna Schwartze

The Trident Trilogy

Eight Years

The Only Reason

Wild Card

The Grand Slam Series

Truth or Tequila

Raine Out

Leave It On The Field

The Blitzen Bay Series

The Runaway Bride of Blitzen Bay

No One Wants That

Pretty Close To Perfect - December 2022 - Preorder on Amazon.

WILD CARD
(THE TRIDENT TRILOGY: BOOK THREE)

DONNA SCHWARTZE

ISBN: 9798741433669

Published by Donna Schwartze, 2021

donnaschwartzeauthor@gmail.com

❀ Created with Vellum

WILD CARD

(The Trident Trilogy: Book Three)

_____

DONNA SCHWARTZE

To Krystal:

Donna Schwartze

For strong women everywhere
who seek and speak the truth.

"Day by day and night by night we were together—all else has long been forgotten by me."

— *Walt Whitman, "Once I Pass'd Through a Populous City"*

Prologue

As he stepped into the room, he saw her lying on the couch. Her beautiful green eyes were open, but he already knew she was dead.

Chapter One

"Millie, will you cut up the veggies for the salad?" Mariel says as she pours herself a glass of wine.

We're at the rental house she and Chase are sharing with Dad. The guys are out buying beer for a party today for Mason's team. Mariel and I have started getting the meal together. Actually, she's started because I'm a horrible cook. Mariel's seen me attempt cooking several times. I'm surprised she's allowing me to help at all.

"Yep," I say, quickly taking a knife off the counter before she changes her mind.

She grabs it back and hands me a smaller knife. "You're chopping vegetables, not taking out an attacker."

We've been back from Pakistan for a few weeks. Since Mason has to be in Virginia Beach for another month, I talked Dad into renting a house here. We're all going to end up back in San Diego but for now, I don't want to be separated from either one of them.

Dad and I will use the time to go back to the Outer Banks and clean out the storage locker where I stashed my grandma's stuff after she died. Mariel flew in to help us. After everything that's happened to me this past year, it's nice having all of my family in one place.

"Chase told me you signed the official papers to resign from the agency. I didn't think your boss would ever accept you leaving. What's his name? George?"

"George retired. I've been dealing with the director, Paul Ward, since Pakistan." I pause for a second, looking around and lowering my voice. I always assume every room's bugged. I wonder if that will ever go away. "Ward's still trying to find the other copy of the video of Alex's death."

"Well, he's going to get it over my dead body," Mariel shouts. She never thinks about bugs. Or maybe she does and she just doesn't care.

"I feel like I'm putting you in danger by having you keep it in your safe deposit box," I whisper. "Maybe you should give it back to me."

"No way. If you or Mack go missing, I'm playing that thing for every media outlet in the world. Everyone's going to know the head of the CIA's Middle East division gave up his most valuable asset. The agency can kiss my ass if they think they can intimidate me. I'll shut the whole place down." She pauses for a second. "Wait, why did George retire? He's not that old, is he?"

"He's only forty-seven, a year younger than Dad."

"So why did he retire so early?"

"Uh, I think with everything that went down with Dad—

you know, George hiding everything from me for all that time. I don't know, maybe he started second-guessing what he was doing with his life. He and his wife are moving to a little beach town in Northern California. He wants to be as far away from D.C. as possible."

"I can't believe you're even talking to him after what he did to you. Mack's pissed that you're going to his retirement party."

"Yeah, Mason is, too. It's the only thing they've agreed on since we got back."

"So why are you going?"

"I don't know. I'm still mad at George, but I've never been much into holding grudges. He and his wife were like family to me when I lived in D.C."

"Well, Chase and Mack are holding enough of a grudge against him to cover all of our bases," Mariel says, laughing.

Ironically, Dad was the one who taught me not to hold grudges. When I was growing up, he told me grudges were like storm clouds moving in on a beautiful sunny day. They could stay for a bit, but then they needed to make way for the sun again.

Dad still feels guilty for disappearing. I think he'd feel better if I was holding a grudge against him, but I forgave him the second I realized he was alive. I don't think I'll ever fully understand why he didn't take me with him, but I'm not mad at him. I'm just so relieved he's back.

"What time's the team coming over again?" Mariel asks as she multi-tasks effortlessly over several steaming pots on the stove.

"Mason said around one, so that means they'll be here about noon," I say. "You know that on-time is late for these guys."

"Yeah, they're a punctual breed. Any more news on when Mason can go back to San Diego? Is that JJ guy working out?"

"I think it's still about a month. And I'm not sure about JJ. Mason won't talk to me about it, which is weird because he shares everything with me."

When Mason agreed to take the team lead back so he could go to Pakistan with me, Culver told him he would be in for at least three months while the guy he was covering for recuperated from an injury. Mason talked him out of that when JJ, Mason's second-in-command, stepped forward to say he would lead the team. Apparently, Culver hesitated a little bit at handing the reins over to JJ. Mason won't tell me why. Culver finally agreed to it only if Mason would stay at least a month to help in the transition.

"Mariel, those onions smell horrible," I say as she drops another handful into a skillet. "They're making me nauseated."

"You said you felt sick the other day, honey." She clicks the fan on the stove hood vent to its highest level. "Do you have a bug?"

"I've been feeling yucky lately. I don't know what it is."

"Are you pregnant?" She turns around to look at me. Her eyes are dead serious.

"I'm not pregnant, Mar," I say, shaking my head. "You know I'm on the pill."

"There's still that one percent chance—"

"I'm not pregnant. Stop." I grab the tomatoes and head over to the sink to wash them. "I'm stressed out about Dad. I'm not sleeping very well. I still can't trust that he's going to be here when I wake up. It doesn't help that I'm not in the same house with him."

"Sweetie, we have an extra room if you want to stay here for a while. You know Mack would like that better anyway."

When Dad left, I was sixteen. He's having a hard time adjusting to me as an adult woman. He especially hates that I'm staying with Mason. And he's not subtle about it. Frankly, he's being an asshole. And that's making Mason act like an asshole, too. They're both so competitive. They've been swarming around me since we got back—attempting to mark their territory. I'm trying to stay out of it, but they're both getting on my nerves.

"No, I want to stay with Mason, but I can't get over here soon enough in the morning to see if Dad's still alive."

Mariel reaches over to take my hand. "You've known he was alive for less than a month. Be patient with yourself. You'll get there."

I squeeze her hand before she heads back over to the stove. "You know, Mar, it doesn't help that you're being an asshole to Dad."

"I will be what I want to be, Millie," she says. "I'm pissed at him. His disappearing act affected Chase and me, too. You're way more forgiving than I am. I want to punish him a little bit."

"Mar—"

"Honey, that's between Mack and me. We both love you.

And down deep, we both love each other. Just stay out of it. We're stubborn people—"

"Huge understatement," I say, rolling my eyes.

"We'll work it out—eventually." Mariel turns around and looks at me. "You know you have to move the knife to chop the vegetables, right? Get to work, princess."

Chapter Two

When we walk into the house, Millie's standing at the kitchen island cutting up tomatoes. I've never seen her do anything that resembles cooking. We're both bad at it. We usually order takeout.

"Babe, you should probably look at the cutting board while you're chopping things," I say as I walk over and pop a carrot into my mouth. "Or maybe just let me do it. You're kind of destroying the tomatoes."

"Mase," she says, smiling. "It's not like you can cook any better than I can."

"No, but I bet I can handle a knife better."

Mack walks up behind me. "Yeah, sweetie. Maybe give Mason the knife."

She holds the knife up—pointing it back-and-forth between us. "Back off. Both of you."

She takes another swipe at a tomato, not taking her eyes off us. "Ahhhh!" she screams as she grabs her hand.

Before we can get around the island to help her, she holds the hand up and smiles proudly. "Just kidding."

Mack shakes his head. "Mason, take the knife away from her."

"Roger that," I say as I take a quick step toward her.

She spins around—pointing the knife at me again. "Try it," she says, taking a step backward.

I reach out swiftly, immobilize her wrist, and grab the knife with my other hand. She jerks her head back in surprise.

"Mase," she says, scowling at me. "You're making my self-defense skills look bad in front of Dad."

"I'm pretty sure he already knew I could get the knife away from you." I kiss the top of her head and wrap her into a hug as I hand the knife to Chase.

"You didn't have to make it look so easy," she whines as she burrows her head into my chest.

"I'm sorry, baby," I whisper into her hair. "I promise I'll act like I'm struggling next time."

"Thank you," she says, puckering her lips for a kiss that I readily give her.

Since we got back from Pakistan, I hate being separated from her for any amount of time. Today, we've only been gone an hour, but I was already getting withdrawal symptoms. Sometimes, I swear I physically feel pain if I go too long without touching her.

"Is there any given second when you two aren't all over each other?" Mack growls from behind us.

Millie tries to pull back, but I press her head to mine for one last slow kiss. I look up to see Mack glaring at me. He's been dropping hints that I'm not nearly good enough for his daughter. Well, not dropping them, more like throwing them at me like grenades. I've been the appropriate amount of respectful, but now he's starting to piss me off. It's not even that I disagree with him, but I'm not going anywhere. He needs to start getting used to it.

"Sorry, Mack," I say, my eyes locked with his. "I keep forgetting where Mack-the-friend ends and Mack-the-father begins."

"It's going to end with my foot in your ass—"

"Dad!" Mille turns around and shoves him in the chest. She's the only person who could do that without losing an arm. "Back off, please. We talked about this."

Mack growls again, muttering something under his breath as he turns around to grab a beer out of the refrigerator.

"He's just jealous because he's not the one getting any for once," Mariel says, looking at Mack with a mischievous smile.

"What do you mean 'for once'?" Millie looks at Mariel, crinkling her nose. "Dad has only had sex one time and that was to create me."

Chase rolls his eyes and lets out a long whistle.

"What does that look mean?" Millie grabs Chase's arm and turns him around. He puts his arms up in protest and shakes his head.

Mack pulls Millie away from Chase. He kisses her forehead. "It doesn't mean anything, sweetie."

Millie looks up at him, frowning. "Wait, Dad . . . Were you a player?"

Mariel busts out laughing as she turns back around to the stove.

"I wasn't a player."

Chase rolls his eyes again and looks down.

"Chase, stop making that face!" Millie pushes his shoulder again.

"Yes, Chase," Mack says, glaring at him. "Stop making that face."

Chase grabs his beer off the counter. "I'm going outside to get the grill ready," he says as he speed walks out the back door.

Millie folds her arms over her chest, shaking her head at Mack. "I can't believe you were a whore. Oh my God. That is way too much information."

"Can we please stop talking about this?" Mack says. "Please."

Mariel turns around and smiles at him. "You know, Mack, you might have an opportunity to get some when we're down in the Outer Banks. I told Carol you were coming down."

Mack steps back like someone just shoved him. He looks from Mariel to Millie.

"Wait, who's Carol?" Millie says, her brow furrowed.

"No one." Mack takes a step toward Mariel. "Mariel, I'm begging you to shut up."

"Carol, sweetie," Mariel says, looking directly at Mack. "Carol Blake."

"Wait. What?" Millie falls back against me. "Like my Aunt Carol? How do you know her?"

"Mariel—" Mack takes another step toward her.

"Yes, Millie. Your Aunt Carol—Chloe's mom." Mariel flashes an evil grin at Mack. "I got to be friends with her when we were living in Virginia Beach."

Millie presses her back harder into me. "But Carol lived in the Outer Banks. How did you meet her?"

Mack leans against the wall, shaking his head as he lets out a long breath.

"Carol came to Virginia Beach every so often to see your dad," Mariel says as she leans back on the counter and crosses her arms.

Millie flips her head to Mack. "What? Did Carol visit you? Like how? As a friend?" Mack's eyes are focused on his feet. "Oh my God, Dad. Were you sleeping with her?"

Mack looks up and takes a quick angry glance at Mariel who's smiling broadly at him.

"Millie," he says, taking her hand and pulling her away from me, "your Aunt Carol and I were dating for a little bit before I left."

"You were dating her aunt?" I laugh and regret it instantly.

Mack flips his head to me. "You might want to sit this one out, boyfriend," he says, his face turning deadly. I've seen several versions of Mack's angry face in the past few weeks, but this one is the most dangerous.

"Yep," I say, grabbing my beer. "What's that Chase? You need help with the grill?"

Chase laughs as I barrel through the back door. "Getting a little hot in there for you?"

"Way too hot. I think Mack's going to kill me one of these nights while I'm sleeping."

"Naw, man. He's just putting you through the wringer a few times," Chase says. "When he left, Millie was a teenager. He's having a hard time adjusting to the fact that she's a woman now. He'll get there."

"He's going to have to because I'm not going anywhere. Maybe it'll get easier if he gets a woman of his own. What's the deal with this Carol?"

Chase pulls up a chair next to me. "Kind of a long story, but short version, she's Millie's best friend's mom. Well, her best friend growing up. I think she kind of lost touch with all of them after Mack died or disappeared or whatever he did."

"Wait. Yeah, Millie's told me about her. A little bit anyway. I think she's the woman who was like Millie's surrogate mom growing up. Right?"

"Yeah, that's what I understand. Mack's mom, Millie's grandma, was pretty worthless, so I think Carol filled in."

"Huh," I say, stroking my beard, "so Mack dated her?"

"Yeah, we didn't talk about it much, but I think they were pretty into each other."

"So why wouldn't he want Millie to know they dated? Millie loves her."

Chase sighs. "I don't know. Mack's complicated. He likes to keep the different parts of his life separated. I don't know if I ever told you I met Millie when she was a baby—right after Mack brought her back from Bosnia—and then not again until she was sixteen. She showed up unannounced on base one day or I wouldn't have met her then. He didn't want her near his work."

"Yeah, I can understand that. He probably didn't want her to worry about him not coming back from a mission and then he didn't come back from one, so . . ."

"Yeah," Chase says, nodding his head. "You know she showed up on base like a week before he disappeared. It was weird like something was guiding her to see him one last time. I remember walking outside to get Mack for a meeting. They were sitting on top of one of those picnic tables in the visitor's area. His arm was around her and her head on his shoulder. She was laughing about something. That image haunted me from the second I thought he blew up in that house."

A flash of déjà vu runs through my head—like I'm seeing her sit on that picnic table. I shake my head to try to get the memory to focus, but it leaves me as quickly as it came.

"Do you know anything about her real mom?"

"Not really," Chase says. "I met her though. Have I told you that? Our team worked with her for a few weeks. She was our translator. That's how they met."

"Does Millie know that?"

He shakes his head. "I'm not sure. After Mack disappeared, I never told her who her real mom was. He didn't want her to know anything about that side of her family because of who her uncle was, you know? She's only known for sure that Nejra was her mom since Sayid told her earlier this year. I guess it's up to Mack what else he shares with her."

I take a long swig of my beer. "People always tell her she looks like her mom. True?"

"Yeah, I guess. It's been so long ago. I don't remember what she looked like, but I remember she was smart and very outspoken, especially for a traditional Muslim woman. And she had a thing for Mack. That much I remember clearly."

"Not so traditional then," I say, laughing.

"Well, you know, we met her in the middle of a war after she had lost both of her parents. As you well know, war changes people. I think she was looking to live a little. I'm sure she thought it was just a matter of time before she died. Sarajevo was being bombed constantly during the siege."

"So were they just together once? Was it a one-night-stand?"

"No, not really. They spent a lot of time working together. I think they developed a mutual affection for each other. Mack liked her—respected her. He tried to move her to the U.S. That was before he even knew she was pregnant. But she didn't want to leave what was left of her family. She was close to her brother and that aunt that just died." He pauses for a second as he grabs another beer out of the cooler. "Mack gave Nejra his address before we left. I was pissed when he told me. As you know, that breaks all kinds of rules, but there was something about her. He felt protective of her. I still don't understand why she didn't contact him to tell him about Millie. She could still be alive today."

He jumps up as Millie walks through the patio door.

"Did you leave Mar and Mack alone in the house?" Chase says, trying to cover the awkward break in our conversation. "One of them is going to kill the other by the end of this month. I'm going to be left without a wife or a best friend."

"It's fine. Dad went to grab something out of the car," Millie says, laughing as Chase hurries inside.

I hold my arms out as she walks over. "Come here, baby," I say as she sits on my lap. She pulls her feet up and curls into a little ball against my chest. "You okay?"

"Yeah, it's weird about Dad and Carol though. I told you about her. She was like a mom to me growing up. I had no idea they had a thing." She takes a deep breath. "I talked to her for the first time in years when I was in the Outer Banks to sell my grandma's house. She was still so sweet, even after years of me blowing her off. I wonder if they'll get back together—"

"Babe, you need to stay out of it," I say, wrapping my arms around her a little tighter.

She looks up at me—eyebrows raised. "Like he stays out of my relationship?"

"He'll leave us alone eventually," I say, nuzzling my nose into her neck. "He's got to figure out a way to be okay with it because I'm never leaving you."

She lays her head back down on my chest. "Promise?"

"Yeah, baby. I promise," I say, kissing her again as I see Mack walk into the yard. "No one's ever getting in between us. No one."

Chapter Three

SARAJEVO, BOSNIA, 1994

"Nejra! You are not going to work outside this house," Sayid said. "And that is my final word."

Since their parents died almost two years ago, Sayid had been trying desperately to get control of his little sister. He thought their father had always been too tolerant of her independence. Now, at twenty-four, Nejra's strong will was almost unmanageable.

"Sayid," Nejra said, looking at him from under her eyelashes like she always did when she wanted to get her way. "I know you are only doing your duty as my brother and the head of this household. I respect your position, but now that you can no longer find work, we need the money."

Sayid shook his head. He knew she was right. When the war started, the jobs dried up quickly. Very few people in Sarajevo had any money to spend. Most of the shops were barely operating anymore.

"If you would just marry Yusef," Sayid said, "he would take care of you. I can fend for myself."

Nejra flung her shoulders back. "I will never marry Yusef. I have told you that repeatedly. I would rather stay single the rest of my life."

Amar smiled as he watched them from the corner of the room. He had been Sayid's best friend since they were three years old. He had been in love with Nejra for almost that long. He knew Sayid didn't see him as a suitable match. Amar's family was poor. Sayid wanted Nejra to have an easy life. Yusef's family was rich, but that's where his qualifications ended. Yusef wasn't nearly smart enough for a woman as brilliant as Nejra.

"Nejra," Sayid said. "You know that's who Papa wanted you to marry. You've been matched with him since you were five."

"Papa wanted me to marry him until Yusef grew up into an ignorant, unfeeling man. Before Papa died, he promised me that I would not have to marry him."

Their parents died in one of the first bombings of the siege. Sayid and Nejra were at work when it happened. When they arrived home that afternoon, they found their Aunt Azayiz stationed in front of what used to be their house. The bombing took out the front wall—next to where their parents sat in the front room with Azayiz's husband. They all died instantly when the wall collapsed on them.

"Well if you're not going to marry him, you have to marry someone," Sayid said. "And please don't tell me again that you're waiting to find a tender man. I've told you before I don't know what that means."

"And I keep telling you I will know him when I meet him and I haven't met him yet."

Amar sat up straight—his heart sinking to his toes.

"If you want to marry a gentle person, then marry Amar," Sayid said, flinging his arms in Amar's general direction. "He has never even been able to kill a bug."

Nejra smiled at Amar. "Amar and I are best friends, but he doesn't want to marry me any more than I want to marry him."

Amar forced a smile onto his face. She was completely wrong about that, but he knew he had to win her over gradually.

"And besides," Nejra continued, "gentle and tender are two different things. Gentle is more of a physical attribute, but tender is something that inhabits someone to their most inner parts. I would welcome gentle, but tender is vital to me."

Sayid shook his head. "I will never forgive Azayiz for giving you that book of poetry. If you show me where it is, I will happily burn it for you."

"I must have lost it," Nejra said, not breaking her stare with him as she sat down at the table.

After the bombing, they moved in with Azayiz. Sayid knew having her in the same household only made Nejra's independence worse. Azayiz and her husband had traveled extensively, including spending a significant amount of time in the United States. Every time they returned from a trip, Azayiz became more westernized and Nejra right along with her.

"Nejra, men are supposed to be tough, not tender," Sayid said, sitting down across from her.

"They can be both," she said, crossing her arms again. "Now about my job, I am supposed to start tomorrow."

Sayid rubbed his hands over his face nervously. "And what does this company do again?"

"They are exporters. They need someone good with languages to help them communicate with all of the different countries of our new region. I speak five languages. I am valuable to them and they will pay me well."

Nejra hated lying to him, but he wouldn't let her work if he knew what she was really going to be doing. One of their father's old friends had contacted her two weeks ago. He said the United States government was sending in envoys to help put an end to the war. They needed a translator who spoke Bosnian, Serbian, Croatian, and English. He knew she spoke all of those languages, in addition to Urdu. She had agreed without even telling her aunt the truth.

"But I don't understand why you will be living there." Sayid knew he would give into her like he always did, but he was holding out hope that she would change her mind. "Why can't you come home at night?"

"We are going to be working late into the evening. You know I can't be out past curfew. There is a barracks just for women. We will report to a woman and have no contact with the men. I will probably be safer there than when I am walking the streets in this neighborhood."

Actually, her father's friend told her she would be working almost entirely with men. He asked her if she would be comfortable with that. Honestly, she didn't know if she would. It frightened and excited her all at the same time.

"And how long will you be there?" Sayid said quietly.

"Only a few weeks, a month at the very most." Nejra smiled at him. She knew she had won.

"You have my blessing on one condition," Sayid said, looking at her sternly. "When the war is over, you will marry immediately."

She smiled and nodded her head. "I promise."

As she got up to walk into the kitchen, she tingled with excitement. It was the first time she felt really alive since the war started.

Chapter Four

MILLIE, VIRGINIA BEACH, VIRGINIA, 2020

"So what's the deal with the tension between your dad and Mason?" Raine says as the door clicks behind the guys heading out to the patio.

We just finished eating. Mariel insisted that Raine and I stay inside for "girl time." Mariel's on her fifth glass of wine. Although she's spaced them out throughout the day, this is still unprecedented. She gets crazy nosy after two glasses, almost insane by three, so this is very dangerous territory.

"What tension?" I say as innocently as I can.

Raine rolls her eyes. "C'mon, Mills. You haven't been out of interrogations that long. I know you haven't lost any of your perception skills."

Mariel smiles at Raine. "I'm going to like you. I can tell that already. Very direct. Yes, Millie, please tell us why your dad and Mason are acting like dogs trying to mark their territory. I wouldn't be surprised if one of them lifts a leg on you soon—"

"Inappropriate!" I point my finger at Mariel. "And disgusting. I'm putting you on lock-down. No more wine."

"Classic avoidance technique—turn the attention back on the questioner." Raine smiles at Mariel.

"Raine," I say, raising my eyebrows. "Don't make me sic Mariel on you."

"Fine," she says, laughing. "We don't have to talk about it —for now."

Mariel sits down opposite us at the table. "So Raine, has Millie told you as little about me as she's told me about you?"

"Pretty much."

"Yeah, she likes to keep all her people separate—just like her dad," Mariel says as she scoops up the last tiny morsel of chocolate cake. "Maybe she should try to keep us better informed about the other people in her life."

"Mar, I've been kind of busy lately. I mean, let's see, in the past month, I've watched my aunt die and watched my boyfriend get shot and almost die. And, then what's that other thing? Oh yeah, I found out my dad was alive after thinking he was dead for nine years. Sorry if I didn't have time to give you a rundown on Raine."

Raine laughs. "Actually, I'm kind of secretive, too. I think when you work at the agency, you're so used to hiding things, you don't talk much about anything."

"Exactly," I say, pointing at Mariel.

"Well we can get to know each other now," Mariel says, turning her attention to Raine. "So Raine, are you dating anyone?"

"No," Raine says. "Frankly, I don't have much time to look."

"Let me look for you—"

"Mariel!"

"Millie, she's a busy working woman who only meets SEALs. I'm just saying it would do our group good if one of us dated outside the fold. We could use some new blood."

"Yeah, I definitely don't want to date any of those guys," Raine says, waving her hand toward the patio. She looks at me. "No offense."

"None taken. Although I still think you should consider Ty's offer. He's so sweet."

"What?" Mariel starts rubbing her hands together feverishly like she's about to hatch an evil scheme. "Ty asked you out? Which one is he? The small one with the adorable curls?"

"No, that's Mouse," I say. "Ty's the quiet one with the really dark hair."

"Ooo, he's cute." Mariel swats my hand away as I try to block her from pouring another glass of wine. "And who can resist the strong, silent type? That's what I noticed about Chase first. All of the other guys on his team—including Mack—actively hunted the women at the bar, but Chase just sat back and observed. I can tell you when he started observing me, it was all I could do not to jump right on top of him and—"

"Oh my God, stop!" I say, throwing my hands over my face.

"Millie doesn't like it when I talk about my sex life with Chase," Mariel says, laughing. "And, she especially doesn't like when I talk about Mack's sex life. And believe me, it was plentiful."

"Mariel," I groan. "My nightmares have completely gone

away since I found Dad. Why are you trying to give me new ones?"

She pats my hand. "Raine, I think you should date outside the teams, but if you're going to sample from the SEAL menu, any of them would be good choices except that JJ guy. What's his deal?"

Raine looks at me to see if she can speak freely. I nod. "Mariel's a vault on professional stuff."

"JJ's always been intense," Raine says, "but lately, he's been off the charts. He's stressed out about being the new team leader."

"Huh," Mariel says. "I don't think he's going to be a good team leader if he can't handle stress. Or a good SEAL at all."

"Oh, he's a great operator," Raine says, "but only with Mason in the lead. They're a strong team. I think JJ's having growing pains—knowing he has to operate without Mason."

"Is that why he hates you so much, Millie?"

"You picked up on that, huh?" I say, shaking my head.

"Kind of hard not to. He straight-out snapped at you when you said hi to him today. What's that about?"

"I have no idea. He's had something against me from the first day I arrived on the base."

"He's protective of Mason," Raine says. "You know, he's the number two, so it's his primary job to take care of number one. That's how the teams are structured. I'm sure that's how Mack was with Chase."

"Yeah, Mack had Chase's back, but he didn't have a problem with Chase dating me. I'm not sure he even thought about it that much."

"Yeah, but would Mack have had a problem if Chase quit the teams to move across the country to be with you?"

"Chase never would have left the teams to be with me. I know he loves me, but Mason's on a different level with Millie. He's completely obsessed." She sees my eyes widen and reaches over to pat my hand again. "But in a good way, honey."

"He's not obsessed with me."

They both roll their eyes.

"Well, I don't know Mason very well yet," Mariel says, "but I can already tell you that he makes his own decisions. It's not Millie's fault he quit the team. So JJ better back off my girl if he's going to be around me. I don't care if he's the size of a whole damn building. I'll still take him out."

"You know, I've never seen you on your sixth glass of wine," I say, laughing. "I guess that's when you reach your delusional stage."

"Okay, first stop counting my drinks like a stalker," Mariel says, pointing at me. "And if I can't take JJ out by myself, Mack's going to help me. After he snapped at you, Mack's eyes didn't leave him. Your dad's a very scary person when he wants to be."

"Well, let's hope it doesn't get to that point—"

Mariel interrupts me. "And I thought it was weird that Mason didn't say anything to JJ. I mean, he was standing right there when JJ snapped at you. I've seen Mason almost take a guy's arm off for accidentally bumping into you. What's that about?"

"They're best friends, Mar," I say, looking at Raine for help. "It's complicated."

"Yeah," Raine says. "I think Mason's trying to manage JJ's stress level. He wants him to be successful as the team lead."

Mariel takes a deep breath. "Again, inability to handle stress is not a good quality for a team leader to have. Chase was in the team lead for almost a decade. I never saw him lose it."

"Yeah, Mason's like ice, too," Raine says. "Hopefully, JJ will get there."

"Yeah, hopefully or he's going to get someone killed," Mariel says, standing up. "We should get outside before Mason comes looking for Millie. I know he can't be apart from her for more than like a few minutes at a time."

Raine laughs. "Damn, Mariel. I'm going to like you, too. That's a spot-on observation."

Chapter Five

After dinner, all the guys are sitting around the patio outside. The ladies are still inside. Mariel insisted on alone time with Millie and Raine. I think they'd both rather be out here with us, but I haven't met anyone who can say no to Mariel.

Chase is showing us the latest sonogram picture of his expected grandchild.

"Aw, man," Ty says to Chase. "You don't look old enough to be a grandpa. When's your daughter due?"

"Two months. She lives in Colorado, so depending on how long we're here, we might stop on the way back and stay there for a while. It's her first kid—our first grandchild. We're all a little anxious."

"Sounds like that kid's about to be spoiled," Hawk says.

"Oh, yeah, I'm going to spoil her so much. I mean, not as much as Mack spoils Millie," Chase says, laughing as he chucks Mack on the shoulder.

"No one has ever spoiled anyone the way Mack spoils Millie," I say into my beer as I take a long swig.

"What's that, boyfriend? You got something to say about the way I raised my daughter?" Mack tilts his head back and roughly rubs his beard. He's got that dangerous look on his face again.

"No, sir. I do not. Your daughter is perfect in every way."

"That's what I thought," he says, nodding slowly.

"It does my heart so much good to see Mason Davis finally scared of someone," Butch says, grinning.

"You mean besides Millie," JJ says, staring right at me.

"Oh!" Everyone recoils in unison, laughing until they see my face.

I look at JJ, shaking my head. "You're not going to leave it alone, are you?"

"I'll leave it alone when you tell your woman what you want."

"Millie knows what I want because it's her." I walk over to him until I'm standing a foot from his chair. "All I want is to grow old with Millie."

"Yeah, that's what she tells you to want."

I'm about to close that final foot of distance between us when a chair comes flying from across the patio and lands with a thud into JJ's knee.

"What's your name? Jay?" Mack says—his leg still pointing toward where he pushed the chair.

JJ snaps his head around to Mack. "JJ—stands for Julius Jackson," he says as he pushes the chair back in Mack's direction—intentionally leaving it short.

"That's my bad. I must have sounded like I cared what

your name is." Mack arcs his beer bottle into the trash can of empties, causing a clank that snaps every head in the backyard to him. "Here's what I do care about: You want to trash Mason? Have at it. But keep my daughter's name out of your mouth."

JJ leans back in his chair and laughs. "Oh yeah? What are you going to do about it, old man?"

"Old man?" Mack sits bolt upright. "Any time you want some of this old man, you let me know. In fact, I think maybe we should go right now."

As he starts to stand up, I leapfrog over a cooler and press his shoulders down. He grabs one of my wrists and almost breaks it with a quick snap.

"Mack!" I say, pulling out of his grip. I tower over him, but make sure I don't touch him again. "I've got this. It's between JJ and me. Stand down."

He settles uncomfortably back into his chair. "Take care of it or I'm going to," he growls with his eyes still fixed on JJ.

I turn back around. "You're being an asshole," I say, pointing at JJ. "Never talk to my father—"

"What? Were you about to call him your father-in-law?" JJ laughs and shakes his head. "Because I thought Millie told you no when you asked her to marry you."

Everyone looks down except JJ who stares right at me.

"What the fuck, man?" I walk over to him.

"What? Didn't everyone know that?" His eyes aren't blinking. He wants this to end badly, but that's not going to happen right now.

Millie and Raine walk through the porch door. Everyone's still looking at their feet. JJ and I are glaring at each other.

"What's going on here?" Millie says, looking at me.

I walk over to her and wrap her into a hug. "Nothing. We were waiting for you to get out here. Butch wants to play poker. I knew you'd want in."

Butch jumps up and starts clearing one of the tables. "Yep," Butch says, throwing his keys to Bryce. "Go get the chips and cards out of the trunk."

"Roger that," Bryce says, hustling out of the back gate.

I glance back at JJ. He's still staring at me, shaking his head. I'm going to have to get into it with him but now's not the time.

I take Millie's hand and lead her over to a chair—pulling her down onto my lap. "How was your girl time?"

"Disturbing, as usual," she says, her forehead scrunched up. "What was that about with JJ? Were you fighting?"

"No, babe, we were just smack-talking. You know how it gets when we're all together."

Her eyes look worried and a little sad. I hate when they look that way. Since the moment I met her, I've done everything I can to make them look happy all the time.

"Are you sure?" she whispers. "I know he doesn't like me, but don't get sideways with him about it. It's no big deal."

"Baby," I say, kissing her forehead, "it's nothing. Really. Don't worry about him. Just concentrate on you and me, okay?"

She nods as she rests her head on my shoulder. I wrap my arms around her and bury my face in her hair as I watch Butch and Bryce set up the poker table. Millie loves to play with them because they've never come close to beating her. She's got the best poker face I've ever seen. It drives Butch crazy.

"Let's go, Mills," Butch says, crooking his finger at her. "It's me, you, Hawk, and Bryce, and the only person who will not win tonight is you."

Millie laughs as she stands up. I give her a pat on her butt. "Go get 'em, baby."

I watch her walk over to the table and then look back at JJ. He's flipping through something on his phone. He's distracted and nervous. Culver told me he wasn't right for the team lead. I convinced him otherwise, but I'm starting to think maybe he was right. JJ's one of the best operators I've ever had on my team. He's been my number two for years. It's the perfect time for him to take the next step, but something's not clicking.

He just went through a nasty divorce. Maybe it's too much change for him. If that's the case, he's going to flip out when I tell him Butch and Hawk are retiring. They're going out at the end of the year—within a few months of each other. They've asked me not to tell him yet. In the long run, it might be a good thing for JJ to get new team members. Hawk and Butch have been on my team since day one. I'm not sure they could take orders from anyone else at this point.

I look back over to Millie. She's laughing as she shoves Butch on the shoulder. Hawk and Bryce start laughing, too. They always light up when they're around Millie—like everyone does, everyone except JJ.

Chapter Six

SARAJEVO, BOSNIA, 1994

Nejra arrived at the abandoned building on the outskirts of Sarajevo exactly at noon. She was nervous but excited. Frankly, she was just glad to be out of her neighborhood. Since the war started, she only made quick trips out to get food and other necessities.

She approached the side door and knocked five times—as instructed. A tall, skinny man with dark hair and glasses opened the door. He looked at her but didn't say anything. She wasn't sure if she was supposed to speak first. Her contact hadn't told her that. He continued to stare.

"My name is Nejra Custovic—"

He grabbed her by the arm and pulled her inside. "Never use your surname. My name is George. I'll be your main contact while you're working with us."

From his accent, Nejra knew he was American. She followed him through the back halls until they arrived at a conference room. There were three people in the room—two women and a man—staring at computer screens. Like George, they were dressed and groomed conservatively.

Nejra was relieved. She expected the worst when she heard she would be working with Americans. She only knew what she saw in movies—brash men and wild women. These people looked nothing like what she expected. They appeared to be as conservative as she was.

"George," one of the computer people said. "The team just arrived."

"Thanks," George said, motioning Nejra toward the door. "Nejra, I want you to meet them. These are the men you'll be working with the most closely."

She nodded and smiled—following him out to the main foyer of the building. When they turned the corner, she stopped so suddenly that she almost lost her balance. Standing before her were six enormous men. They had long hair and scraggly beards. Most of them were wearing short-sleeved T-shirts that revealed a myriad of tattoos trailing down their arms. They had rifles slung across their bodies and pistols at their waists.

"This is Nejra. She's our translator," George said. "She speaks about every language, so she'll be valuable. Nejra, you don't have to remember their names, but they're Chase, Mack, Harry, Clem, Jag, and Mick."

She nodded to the team—trying not to show her unease with their virile appearance. The only men she saw regularly were her brother and his friends. They were very tidy, small men. These men looked like wild beasts to her. One of them lifted his T-shirt to wipe his face, revealing his bare stomach. Nejra looked away quickly.

She thought she might faint out of extreme embarrassment.

"Nice to meet you, ma'am," Chase said, taking a few steps toward her. "Your main contact will be Mack. When we need to get information out of someone, he's our go-to guy. You can translate for him."

Chase motioned toward Mack who took a step forward.

"Ma'am," Mack said, smiling at her. "Thank you for being here. I'm afraid I only speak English."

"And you barely speak that," Clem said, laughing.

Mack shook his head as he looked over at Clem. He glanced back at Nejra and smiled again to try to make her feel more comfortable. He couldn't help but notice how anxious she looked. "I'll try to keep up with you, ma'am," he said. "Let me know if I can do anything for you."

She gave him just a glimmer of a smile as she turned around to follow George across the room. Mack watched her walk away. She was probably only five-four with a very slight build. Her clothes were too big for her. She looked uneasy in them. She left the top two buttons of her shirt open. Mack guessed by the way she was pulling at her collar that she was uncomfortable with that decision. She had her long, brown hair pushed behind her ears, causing her big, dark-green eyes to jump out of her face. She was beautiful, but her eyes—like the rest of her—looked tired. He could tell the war had been hard on her.

Nejra looked back at Mack and was surprised when she saw him still looking at her. He looked away and followed the team into their ready room to unpack. She watched him walk away. He was slightly taller than the rest—probably a little over six feet. He had bushy dark red hair and a long, scraggly beard to match. His eyes were green but much lighter than hers. They were almost the color of the lemongrass tea her mother used to make before the war. He looked older than her, except when he smiled and his eyes sparkled like a mischievous teenager. Nejra liked when he smiled. It had made her feel a little less uneasy. Despite his almost dangerously masculine appearance, she felt instantly comfortable with him.

"Nejra." She turned around to see George looking at her. "You'll go out with the team tomorrow. Mack can get you ready today."

"Get me ready?" she said slowly.

"Download you on the operation—tell you what to expect," George said, narrowing his eyes. "Get you fitted for a protective vest and helmet."

Nejra's mouth gaped. She hadn't thought she was going to leave this building.

George took a step toward her. "Didn't you know you were going to work in the field?"

She recovered quickly. "Yes, of course, I did. I didn't know it would be so soon. Where would you like me to work today?"

George led her into an empty conference room. Mack was already seated at the table. He stood up when she walked in and pulled out the chair next to him, smiling warmly again and motioning for her to sit down. Nejra paused for a second as a warm sensation rushed through her body.

Mack pushed her chair in as she sat down—being very careful not to touch her. He saw her panicked look when George walked out, leaving them alone in the room.

Mack smiled at her again. "I know this is probably difficult for you," he said. "Please tell me what I can do to make
you more comfortable. Would you feel better if someone else
was in the room with us?"

She shook her head as she looked up into his gentle eyes.
She thought she could probably get lost in them forever.

"I know I look rough," Mack said, "but you're safe with
me. I promise. I would never do anything to make you feel
uncomfortable. Just talk to me and let me know if something's
not working for you. Okay?"

"Okay," she said as he turned his laptop screen to her.

As Mack explained what her duties would be, she thought
about what Sayid said—that a man couldn't be both tough and
tender. She told him it was possible for a man to be both. Her
body tingled with excitement when she realized she might
have just met such a man.

Chapter Seven

MILLIE, VIRGINIA BEACH, VIRGINIA, 2020

"There ain't a chance you got that other queen, Millie." Butch relaxes back in his chair, spreading his legs wide. He nods his head at me while he gnaws on a toothpick. He's the picture of confidence except for his right eye. It's twitching. I would think a SEAL would know never to play poker with a CIA interrogator. We pick up on everything.

"Yeah, so you've said about twenty times. If you don't think I have it, then call, and let's get on with our lives." He has a full house showing with three aces. I have three queens showing. The only way I can beat him is with four of a kind. I'm holding his other ace. He's not holding the other queen.

"Mason! Tame your woman!" Butch spits out the toothpick as he snarls in Mason's general direction.

"Not a chance," Mason says from behind me where he's sitting with Dad and Chase. "I like her wild."

I hear Dad's low growl. "Haven't I asked you repeatedly

not to say things like that in front of me?" I turn around to find him shaking his head at Mason whose eyes are fixed on me.

"You have, brother. You have." Chase pats Dad on the shoulder.

I turn back to Butch. "Good lord, Butch. I hope it doesn't take you this long to make a decision in the field."

Bryce laughs from the seat to my right. "There's a reason we never let him go into a room first."

"Rookie, you know you better keep that mouth shut unless you want Uncle Butch to give you an ass-whooping." Butch is still trying to read me. He hasn't gotten close all night. No one has. Bryce and Hawk folded two rounds ago.

"I'm not the rookie anymore, dumbass. Matt's been with us for almost a month. Try to keep up."

Butch moves his eyes slowly off me and looks behind him where Matt's sitting with Ty and Mouse by the fire pit. "Young Matthew, you graduated from college. Bring some of that fancy book learning over here and tell me what to do."

Matt doesn't move anything except his eyes which shift to me. "Wasn't she a CIA interrogator?"

"She was," Butch says slowly.

"Then don't you think she can probably read you way better than you can read her?"

"That's not helpful at all." Butch looks at Hawk. "That's why the youth should be seen and not heard."

Hawk shakes his head. "You've got to pull the trigger, brother. Call or fold."

Butch looks over my shoulder. "Mack, you know her best. What do you think?"

"I think your rookie's smarter than you and it's not even

close." I'm not looking at Dad, but I can tell he's smiling proudly at me.

"Fuck!" Butch throws his cards on the table. "I fold. Show me the queen."

"You're looking at her," I say as I flip my two cards face up—an ace and a ten. No queen.

"Damn!" Bryce slaps his hand on the table. "She bluffed you right out of your shorts."

"I hate you so much right now," Butch says, glaring at me.

"That's rude," I say as I push my chair back.

"And hateful." Hawk pats my hand.

"Yes, and hateful. Thank you, Hawk," I say, wiping away non-existent tears. "Now, I believe you threw your watch into the pool last round. Should we get it from your car before you forget?"

Butch pushes himself up. "Does someone want to come with us to make sure I don't kill her?"

"Naw," Mason says as he pulls me down to his level for a kiss. "The way she just whipped your ass, I'm guessing she can beat you in just about any fight at this point."

"Let's go, Millicent," Butch says, pulling me away from Mason.

"Okay, Gabriel." Butch snaps his head around to me. "What? You don't think I know what your real name is?"

I hear the guys laughing behind me as Butch continues to pull me to the gate.

"That is my great-grandaddy's name and it's completely manly."

"Good, then you won't mind if I start calling you that all the time."

Butch looks up at the sky. "Good Lord, you never gave me a little sister when I was young. Why have you cursed me with one now?"

He puts his arm around my shoulder and pushes me through the backyard gate toward the front of the house. He's babbling on about his watch being an heirloom and how he won't be able to function without it. I'm shaking my head and laughing until we round the corner.

Paul Ward, the director of the CIA, is standing in the front yard. There's an armored limo behind him surrounded by his protective detail—four men in dark suits and sunglasses. For a split second, I think I'm dreaming—or having a nightmare in this case.

"Oh hell no!" I say as I come to a quick stop.

Butch yanks me behind him and pulls a pistol out of his waistband. The four guys with the director step in front of him and pull their weapons on us. All of a sudden, we have a standoff in the middle of sleepy Virginia Beach.

"Butch!" I say, trying to step around him. He blocks me with his arm. "Why are you carrying a weapon at a barbecue?"

He nods his head toward the director. "They're carrying weapons. Why don't you ask them the same question?"

"They're federal agents protecting the CIA director."

"And I'm a Navy SEAL protecting a poker cheater," he drawls out slowly. "I don't see much difference."

The director steps around his men. "She cheats at poker?" he says, grinning.

"Like a professional." Butch blocks me again as I try to get around him.

"No, I don't cheat at poker, he just can't read a bluff to

save his life," I say directly into Butch's ear. He swats my face away. I look back at the director. "Why are you in my front yard?"

The director looks at his detail and motions for them to put their guns away. They do so hesitantly.

"Put your gun away, Butch," I say, placing my hands on his shoulders. "It's okay. Really."

"I'll put it away," he says, tucking it into his front waistband. "But you stay behind me."

"George told me you're dating a SEAL," the director says, nodding his head toward Butch, "but this can't be him—"

"Why can't this be him?" Butch says and then lets out a long whistle. "I mean, that's downright hurtful."

The director smiles. "And I know this isn't your dad. I've never met him, but I've seen pictures. Is he here? I'd like to talk to him."

"You're not getting anywhere near my dad," I say, glaring at him. "Butch, take your gun back out."

"No need. Turn around, Mills," Butch says, laughing. "Turn around."

Chapter Eight

Millie and Butch have barely cleared the gate to the front yard when I hear Butch's whistle. If our radios aren't working on a mission, we've developed all kinds of sounds to signal different situations. That whistle is his danger warning. Everyone on my team jumps up in unison and grabs our pistols out of our waistbands.

The team looks at me for instruction. After years of leading them, it's their first instinct. JJ looks pissed, but he's looking at me, too. I use hand signals to send Ty and JJ wide right, Bryce to the roof, and the rest to follow me to the gate. Chase and Mack fall in line like they're still active. They're not carrying weapons. I guess that's a retirement thing. I wonder if I'll ever feel comfortable without a gun strapped to my side.

Hawk goes through the gate first with me following. We hug the side of the house until we can get a good look. Butch has his gun drawn on what looks like four feds. Butch's other arm has Millie pinned behind his body. She's looking at an older man standing in front of an armored vehicle.

Millie's wriggling around—trying to loosen Butch's grip on her. She says something I can't hear, but Butch replies, "Turn around, Mills."

She turns around to see us spread out behind them—guns drawn. She glances up to the roof and sees Bryce sprawled out on overwatch. When I get over to them, she's shaking her head.

"Seriously?" she yells. "You guys are really at a barbecue with weapons?"

"Is that a weird thing?" Hawk says, taking her arm from me and dragging her back to where Chase and Mack are leaning against the fence, observing the action.

I turn around and walk toward the older man. "How can I help you?"

He looks up at me, smiling. "You must be her boyfriend. I knew it wasn't him," he says, gesturing toward Butch.

"Again, very hurtful," Butch says.

Millie makes her way back over to us with Mack in tow. "Mason, Dad, this is Paul Ward. He's the director of the agency. What he's doing here, I don't know."

"So you're Mack Marsh," Ward says, walking forward and extending his hand. "I've always wanted to meet the guy who caused me so much trouble."

Mack declines his hand. "If you're here for me, let's get to it. I'm not much for small talk."

Millie tries to step in front of Mack. We both block her and push her behind us.

"I'm not here to see you," Ward says. "That business is

thankfully behind us. I'm here to see your daughter. We still have some unfinished business."

"The hell you do—"

"Dad," Millie says, trying to wedge her body between us so she can see Ward. "It's fine. Can I please handle this?"

Ward laughs at Millie as she struggles to get in front of us. I wonder how much time I'd serve for smacking the director of the CIA.

"Millie, do you always roll with this much protection?" Ward says. "You're making my detail look bad."

We finally let Millie through us, but we each have a hand on one of her shoulders, preventing her from walking too far forward.

"What do you want? What unfinished business?" Millie says, shimmying to try to get our hands off her shoulders. It doesn't work.

"I would like to tell you privately. Maybe we can sit in my car and talk," Ward says, taking a step closer to her. Mack and I both pull her back.

She whips around and looks back and forth between Mack and me. "Would you stop? Please. I'm fine."

She turns around to face Ward again. "I'll talk to you, but first, your guys give up their weapons while we're in the car."

Ward's head man walks forward, shaking his head.

"That's fine," Ward says, stopping the man with his hand in the air. "We're all on the same team here."

Millie turns around. "Hawk, Butch, take their weapons and search them."

Hawk and Butch spring forward and start patting them down.

Mack laughs and looks over at me. "Does she always try to run your team like this?"

"Nope, this is a first," I say, grinning as I look down at Millie.

"Sorry," she says, biting her lip.

"No, please. You're doing a great job. Continue," I say, putting my gun back in my waistband.

She rolls her eyes, but continues, "Who's your driver? He gives his keys to Mason."

Ward nods at a guy who reluctantly steps forward and hands me the keys.

"Did I miss anything?" Millie says, looking up at me.

Mack and I are still laughing. "We'll search the inside of the car before you get in, but A-plus for effort, babe."

Ty heads over to the car when I signal him. One of the feds tries to step in front of him, but he knows he's worthless without his weapon. As Ty crawls into the back of the limo, I pull Millie back a few steps. Mack and Chase join us.

"Millie, you need to have one of us in there with you," Chase says.

"C'mon, Chase. You remember how Paul works. He's not saying anything to me unless we're alone."

Mack turns her toward him. "If he tries to overpower you, can you take him?"

"Dad," she says, sighing. "He's a hundred years old. Of course, I can take him."

"We don't know what kind of training he has—"

"He was an analyst before he got this position. He's a pencil pusher. I've got this. Plus, even if he could take me—which he can't—what's he going to do next? He has no weapons, no backup. And why in the world would he want to harm me? I mean, to what end?"

She's using her controlled but annoyed voice. When I hear that voice, I back off immediately.

"Don't use that tone with me, Millie," Mack says, getting down on her eye level. I guess dads aren't as scared of that voice as boyfriends are. "I will physically restrain you if I have to. I'm giving you five minutes in that car and then we're coming for you."

She takes a deep breath and nods. I wonder if Mack would teach me how to control her like that.

"Mase, the car's clean," Ty says, walking up to us. "And I searched the old guy. He's clean, too."

"Okay," I say, following Millie as she walks toward the car.

"Five minutes, Millie," Mack says from behind us.

I walk to the car and open the door for Millie. Ward looks up at me, "This is a private conversation."

"For now it is," I say as I close the door behind him.

Chapter Nine

SARAJEVO, BOSNIA, 1994

"Does your family live in the city?" Mack asked.

They had been working together in the conference room for about an hour. It had only taken Nejra a few minutes to feel comfortable with him. His deep, calm voice was almost hypnotic to her.

"I live with my brother," she said. "My parents were killed at the beginning of the war."

"I'm sorry to hear that," he said softly. "Were you close to them?"

Nejra looked up at him with confusion in her eyes. "Of course I was close to my parents. Aren't you?"

Mack sighed and shook his head. "My dad was out of the picture before I was born. My mom blames me for it. She's not a very nice person."

"That sounds difficult," Nejra said, looking down. "I'm sorry."

"Not nearly as difficult as what you've been through—"

"I don't know if that's true. I had perfect parents for twenty-two years. I feel lucky to have had them at all."

He smiled at her. "They were good people?"

She smiled back even though she had been taught not to smile at men. It felt so natural with him. "They were the best people. My mother was lovely, strong, and passionate. And my father was smart, quiet, and probably much too tolerant of his headstrong daughter."

Mack grinned as she laughed. She finally seemed like she was settling down a little bit.

"You know it's the father that guides a daughter's confidence," she said as she twirled the ends of her hair around her finger. "The bond between mother and daughter is unbreakable, but the father—how he treats his daughter—determines how she will let other people treat her when she's an adult. At least, that's how it was for me. My father made sure I knew how a woman should be treated—how she should be respected."

Mack nodded. "I'm glad he gave you that confidence. Men should treat you with respect."

Nejra was surprised and thrilled he was listening to what she said. She never talked this openly with any man, including her brother.

"Do you have any kids?" she asked. She wasn't sure why she was hoping the answer would be no.

"No wife. No kids. This job makes it a little hard to have either."

"You should have kids," she said, releasing the breath she

had been holding in. "You would be a good father to a daughter, despite the way you look."

"Wait, what?" Mack's hearty laugh rebounded off the walls of the small room. "Do I have to be good-looking to be a good dad?"

She raised her eyebrows and looked at him almost coyly. "You are very handsome. You know that. I mean the way you are, uh . . . What's that word? I think it's a Spanish word, umm —machismo. You have strong machismo."

"I don't speak Spanish—"

"You know—macho, tough," she said, making a muscle with her very slim arm. "You are that way on the outside, but underneath, I sense you are a tender person."

"I don't know about that—"

"I do. I can see it in you," she said, nodding. "If you ever have a daughter, treat her insides tenderly, but make her strong on the outside. It's what my father did for me, and I think it's served me well."

"Yes it has," he said. "I'm not sure if I'll ever have kids. It's not in my plans right now. Do you want kids?"

"Yes," Nejra said. "Well, I did. The war changed so much. Before it started, I wanted to get married and raise a family. Now, I'm not so sure—especially with my parents dying. War makes you think a lot about how short life can be."

When he saw her eyes tear up, Mack put his hand on top of hers. She jerked her hand away.

Mack jumped back and pushed his chair away from her. "I'm so sorry, ma'am. That was just instinct. I shouldn't have touched you. I know better."

"No. It's m-my fault," she said, trying to control the redness that was coming to her cheeks. "You just surprised me. I know you didn't mean any harm. And please call me Nejra."

"Yes, ma'am," Mack said, standing up. "I think we're done. Again, I apologize."

"There is no need. Really." Nejra smiled at him. "George told me you would fit me for some equipment I will need tomorrow. I think he said a vest and helmet."

"Yes, ma'am," Mack said as he squeezed by her—his back pressed firmly against the wall. "I'll send one of our analysts in—one of our female analysts—to help you with that."

"I am sorry I have made you uncomfortable," Nejra said, panic rising in her voice as she realized he was leaving. "Please call me Nejra. We will be working together. And what should I call you?"

"You can call me Mack," he said, looking down. "Or stupid because that's how I feel right now."

She smiled broadly again. "You are not stupid. You are the opposite of that. You are a warm and lovely person. I've enjoyed talking to you. Maybe we can talk again—"

"Yes, ma'am. Maybe," Mack said, nodding at her one more time before he turned around to leave the room. "I need to get going now."

Nejra watched him disappear through the door. The tingling sensation rushed through her body again. Somehow she knew, deep in her soul, that she wanted him to be the one. As the war dragged on, she realized her time in this life might be limited. She had thought for months about things she wanted to experience before she died. Being with a man was one of those things. She ignored the feeling because there were no men in her life that interested her in that way—until today.

Chapter Ten

MILLIE, VIRGINIA BEACH, VIRGINIA, 2020

As I get into the car, I take the seat opposite the director and stare at him—my arms crossed. He stares back with a slight smile on his face.

"You're not scared of much, are you?" He squints at me like he's trying to figure out what I'm thinking.

"I'm not scared of you if that's what you mean. What do you want? You're not getting the tape if that's why you're here, so quit asking."

"You're putting yourself in danger by holding onto it—"

I glare at him. "You have no idea what I'm willing to do to protect my dad. If you come for him—or me—that tape's going to be heard by everyone. You'll never be able to recruit another informant."

He sighs and shakes his head. "I do want that tape, but that's not why I'm here. Amar Petrovic is missing."

"Okay," I say slowly. "Last I heard, he and his wife moved

to Rome. Is he an official missing person? Seems like that would be a police problem."

"We've been tracking him—"

"For what possible reason?" I say. "He was never involved in the network. He just had the bad fortune to grow up on the same street with Sayid and Yusef."

"We thought that at first, but now we're not too sure. He's always been the wild card in this situation."

"He's not a wild card," I say, shaking my head. "He's not any kind of card. He's a dentist."

"You know we've been pouring through your uncle's journals since he died. You were there that day. You saw how many there were. He recorded everything. He refers to someone in the journals as "Mir." The best we can make out, it's the person who was running the network's ground game. You know, taking care of their business affairs in broad daylight while the fighters were hiding in the mountains."

"I know what "ground game" means, Paul." He flinches when I call him by his first name, but then smiles. "Amar wasn't running anyone's ground game. Again, he's just a dentist."

"It's a good cover—"

"It's not a cover. I had Amar under observation for months before we went in and grabbed him for an interview. He never did anything suspicious—"

"Except talk to your uncle on burner phones!"

"I talked to him about that. He said Sayid was rambling on those calls. Best I can make out, Sayid knew he was dying and he wanted to relive old childhood memories."

"Really, Millie? Come on. You're not that naive. You think

one of the world's deadliest terrorists suddenly wants to talk about the old times?"

"Yeah, you know what, I do. I talked to Sayid. You didn't. I mean, he developed into a ruthless killer, but my read was that he wasn't always like that. I think losing his entire family changed him. And yeah, maybe at the end of his life, he wanted to feel like the person he was when he was younger."

"That's BS. Maybe you want to think that because you were his niece."

"Look, Paul, no offense—"

He laughs. "We crossed that bridge the first time we met. I don't think either one of us cares if we offend the other."

"Fair enough. You're a bureaucrat. You haven't been in the trenches and don't know the first thing about reading someone. I do and I'm good at it. Amar's a dentist—nothing else."

He nods his head as he tries to get a read on me again. He's worse at it than Butch is and I didn't think that was possible.

"Are we done?" I say.

"We brought Amar's wife in for questioning. She won't talk to anyone except you. She says she knows you."

"She doesn't know me. I met her briefly when we brought Amar in for questioning in Sarajevo. We ended up moving them to Portugal so Sayid couldn't find them. He found them anyway."

"Wonder how that happened?" He rolls his eyes. "Amar and Sayid were still in touch. You said in your report that Sayid was trying to find you after that shootout in the mountains. At the time, you thought Amar was trying to help you find Sayid. Actually, I think he was trying to help Sayid find you."

"Whatever. We found each other. Sayid's dead. I don't care what Amar's motivations were. You accepted my resignation —finally. Let's move on."

"I need you to go to Rome and talk to the wife."

"No."

"Millie, don't make me force you."

"Really?" I say, gesturing toward the window. "You and what army? I know you saw the protection I have out there."

"I have a video, Millie," he says, his bottom lip quivering. "It's of you and Agent Laskin having sex in your hotel room in Pakistan. I would hate for your boyfriend to see it."

"That's what you're going with?" I say, laughing. "You know damn well I didn't sleep with Alex in Pakistan."

He smiles. "I said I have video of you having sex with him. I believe you know what that means."

I shake my head and start toward the limo door. He grabs my arm and tries to pull me back to my seat.

"Get your hand off me or you're leaving here with a broken arm," I say as I open the door. I look over my shoulder at him and smile. "You know I can and will break it. Last warning."

He removes his hand slowly. "Millie, please don't leave. We need to finish this conversation."

"I'm not leaving," I say without looking at him. I poke my head out of the door. "Mason, will you join us, please?"

Mason covers the ten feet between us in one step. I sink back into my seat. Mason looks into the car and gives Paul a long, hard stare before he crawls in and sits next to me—closing the door behind him.

"What do we have here?" Mason says as he puts his hand on my knee.

"The director says he has a video of Alex and me having sex in Pakistan," I say, smiling up at Mason. "He would like to show it to you."

Mason sits up straighter and wraps his arm around my shoulder. He's glaring at Paul. "Is that right? Well I would like to see that."

"Millie," Paul says, looking from Mason to me. "You know what I have."

"Yes, I do. Mase, the agency's very talented at making fake videos to blackmail people into talking—insanely talented. They hire actors that look just like the people they're trying to blackmail."

"Interesting," Mason says, rubbing his beard. "Well, let's look at it. Frankly, I want to see who you got to play Millie. And let me tell you, her ass better be amazing because Millie's is the best I've ever seen."

"Aww, baby, thank you," I say, snuggling into his chest. He kisses the top of my head.

Paul shakes his head. "Let's forgo the video. He can leave now."

Mason laughs. "Naw, I just got all comfortable," he says, pulling me closer to him. "Why don't you catch me up?"

"The agency thinks Amar Petrovic was working with my uncle's network—"

"Millie!" Paul reaches over to stop me. Mason grabs his

wrist and twists it almost to the point of breaking. Paul cries out and pulls it back when Mason releases it.

I look from Paul's shocked face to Mason's deadly face. "They want to question him, but he's gone missing. His wife says she'll only talk to me. They want me to go over to Rome —where Amar and his wife are living now—and try to get her to tell us where he is."

"Petrovic? The guy we picked up in Sarajevo?" Mason doesn't take his eyes off Paul.

"Yeah. He called Dad about me when I was a baby and then warned him about Yusef coming after me just before Dad disappeared."

Mason looks down at me. "Do you think he was working with Sayid?"

"Not a chance."

"Then we're done here," Mason says, reaching for the door.

"Not quite," Paul says, raising his arm, but making sure to keep it far away from Mason. "There's something else I need to tell Millie about Amar and I think she'd probably like to hear it privately."

Chapter Eleven

MASON, VIRGINIA BEACH, VIRGINIA, 2020

Paul Ward is staring at Millie gravely—like he's about to reveal the deepest secrets of the universe.

"Do you want me to go?" I say to Millie as I pull her a little closer.

"No. Stay." Her face is void of all expression, but I can tell she's a little apprehensive by the way she's squeezing my hand. "Paul, enough drama. Say what you're going to say."

"You said you'd do anything to protect your dad. I'm just wondering which one. We have reason to believe Amar Petrovic is your biological father."

"Man, shut the fuck up," I say, shaking my head. "You people will say anything to get what you want."

Millie starts rubbing her temples. "You're the worst," she says, looking up at him. "Seriously, you're worse than George. Amar Petrovic is not my father."

"I'm just saying there's a possibility—a good possibility."

She leans further into me as she sighs and looks up at

Ward. "There's not a good possibility; not a bad possibility. There's no possibility."

I'm glaring at Ward. He looks at me and then back to Millie. "According to Sayid's journal, your mother married Amar just before she died."

"Well, then he was going to raise another man's baby because Mack Marsh is my dad. I mean, you saw him?" she says, pulling her strawberry-blonde ponytail to the front. "Where do you think I got this hair?"

"And your ears are identical," I say, tilting her head so I can look at one.

"Seriously?" she says, laughing as I examine her ear. "How did you even notice that?"

"I don't know. I was talking to Mack one day and noticed. He has small ears for a guy his size," I say, quickly adding, "Please don't tell him I said that or that I even looked at his ears."

She shakes her head and laughs. "Okay, this conversation is getting ridiculous. It's over."

"Millie," Ward reaches his hand out toward her and then pulls it back when he sees my face. I think it would be a good idea for him to learn how to talk without using his hands. He looks back at Millie. "I'll fly you over on one of my private jets. I'll put you up in a luxury villa. You'll be in and out in a day—two days tops. It's Rome for fuck's sake. You just have to talk to Amar's wife for a few minutes. You can spend the rest of the time eating pasta and drinking wine."

"I'm not on your payroll anymore," Millie says. I can tell she's considering going.

"Then I will pay you a consultant's fee."

She stares at him for a few seconds. "I want the highest fee you pay anyone and Mason comes with me."

"Agreed," he says. "I'm going to send Raine Laghari with you, too. And I'd like to send a few more SEALs just in case we have to grab Petrovic."

"My team can come with us," I say, looking down at Millie. "If you want to do this, Mills. Do you trust him?"

"Sitting right here," he says. I ignore him.

"Yeah, he's fine. I know he's lying about Amar being my father, but Amar's the one who got me to Dad, so let's go over there and see if we can find him. And Rome's a romantic city—"

"Again, I'm right here," Ward says, shaking his head.

Millie looks back at him. "Yeah, we'll go."

He sits back, looking satisfied. "Good. Master Chief, I don't need your entire team. Pick two guys. We have to run low on this. I need you to blend in as much as possible."

"Butch Harrison and Hawk Fuller."

Millie looks up at me, smiling. "Those are the two guys you choose to blend in?"

"JJ's trying to take the reins of the team. Hawk and Butch are retiring at the end of this year. He's going to have to replace them eventually. It might as well be now."

Ward nods. "We'll start working on that today. Millie, my office will call you with the details, but it's probably going to take them a day to get the Navy to pull these guys off their team."

"Captain Harrison Culver is your guy," I say to Ward. "He'll approve it."

"Good," Ward says. "Plan on wheels up Monday morning."

Millie nods as I open the door for her. As we crawl out, we see my team still spread out in their watch positions. I nod to Chase. "You can give them back their keys. We're done."

Chase throws the driver his keys and follows Mack over to us.

"What was all that?" Mack says. "Are you in trouble because of me?"

"No, nothing like that. You remember Amar Petrovic?" she whispers. "He's missing. They think he might have had some involvement in Sayid's network. Since I know the most about the network, they want me to go over to Rome to question a few people."

She's leaving out key details, especially the part about the agency thinking Amar might be her father. From the look on Mack's face, I don't think he's picking up on it. He's good at reading her, but he doesn't have much experience when she activates agent-mode.

"Sweetie, you don't work for them anymore," he says. "You don't have to help them out."

"I know, but it's just a few days and they're paying me a lot. Mason's going with me." Mack looks up at me with relief in his eyes. "But, I don't want to leave you for even two days, Dad."

Mack looks back at her. "Mills, that should be the least of your worries. I'm going to be here when you get back."

"But we were going down to the Outer Banks next week to go through Camille's stuff—"

"Chase and Mar will help me. You took care of everything while I was gone. Let me take care of stuff now."

Millie nods. "Okay."

"Hey," I say, putting my arm around her. "Can I talk to you for a second?"

Mack eyes me suspiciously as I pull her away.

She looks up at me. "What? You don't want to go anymore?"

"I'm going," I say and then whisper, "Are you going to tell Mack what the director said about Amar being your dad?"

"No." Her eyes narrow. "And that's my decision, Mason."

"It's the wrong decision. You need to tell him."

"No, I don't. It'll just upset him. Amar's not my father."

"I know he's not," I say. "That's not the point. You need to tell Mack."

"I'm not going to—final decision." She tries to get around me, but I block her. "Mase, leave it alone."

I tilt her chin up to look at me. "You know, I used to think you hid information from people because you had trust issues, but I don't think that's it anymore. I think you hold it back because you're trying to protect people from themselves."

"I don't do that," she says, looking over at Mack.

"Yeah, you do." I step aside so she can get around me. "Maybe one day you'll realize we can protect ourselves."

She looks over her shoulder at me as she walks back to Mack. "My decision, not yours."

"Everything okay?" Mack puts his arm around her and looks at me. "What was that about?"

"Nothing. He was asking me about something the director said about one of our targets."

He leans down and looks at her. I'm hoping he can tell she's lying, so he'll force the truth out of her. "Is the target dangerous?"

"He's not dangerous," she says, smiling up at him.

"Okay." He puts his arm around her, looks at me one more time, and starts walking to the backyard. "C'mon, let's get back to the party. I think Butch still has a few pennies in his pocket you need to take from him."

She laughs as she puts her arm around his waist. "Do you remember when we played poker when I was little? You always looked at my hand and gave me what I needed so I could win."

"Yeah and you always wanted to collect only the queens," he says, flipping her ponytail. "I'd deal you five cards—and even if you had four aces—you'd want to replace them all if you didn't have any queens."

I watch them walk through the gate. Millie's looking up at him—giggling like she's five years old. I've never heard her make that sound. It sounds like pure happiness. Maybe she's right about not telling him. Their relationship might finally be getting back to where it was before he disappeared. I don't think there's any way he's not her biological father, but if she ever found out he wasn't, I truly think it might break her.

Chapter Twelve

SARAJEVO, BOSNIA, 1994

"Who are we hunting for tonight?" Nejra whispered to Mack as the team got ready to leave.

Mack attempted to smile. She knew he was trying to calm her down, but she noticed his usually gentle eyes had turned hard and cold.

"Some bad guys," he whispered.

"But—"

He looked down at her. "Stay close to me—like we practiced. That's all you need to do, okay?"

She nodded as the team started crawling into the back of the van. Clem offered Nejra his hand to help her in, but Mack knocked it away. She climbed up herself with the help of the door handle. She noticed Mack's arms were at the ready behind her in case she fell. She looked around nervously, as the men spread out all over the floor. She wasn't sure where to sit.

"You need to be in the middle. It's safer in case we're

attacked," Mack said. When he saw her wide eyes, he added, "We're not going to get attacked. You're fine."

Despite her climbing anxiety, Nejra almost laughed out loud as she sat down. Only a day before, Mack had been embarrassed when he touched her hand. Now, she was in the middle of six men—their enormous arms and legs touching her from all sides. She didn't feel threatened after Mack made one of the other guys move so he could sit next to her.

Nejra closed her eyes and tried to figure out where they were going. She felt the van climbing, so she figured they were going into the mountains. She knew that was not a very safe place to be right now. The Serbs were launching the bombings into Sarajevo from there. Her body shuddered as she realized they were probably hunting Serbian leaders.

"Just stay close to me," Mack whispered again as he felt her body shake against his. "I won't let anything happen to you."

Nejra nodded again. As the van started taking hairpin turns, she was finding it hard to sit upright. She leaned her body up against Mack to steady herself. He didn't push her away and after the van took a particularly wild turn, she felt his arm go around her waist. The tingling sensation shot through her body again.

After about twenty minutes, the van stopped. Harry opened the doors to reveal a small mountain village.

"Nejra," Chase said, leaning down to look into her eyes. "Stay close to Mack. Go wherever he goes."

She nodded—trying to hide her anxiety as it skyrocketed through her body. As the team walked slowly toward the village, Mack took her hand and placed it through a loop hanging from his belt.

"Don't let go," he said as he dropped his night-vision goggles into place.

They had barely gotten into the village when a building exploded about a hundred feet ahead of them.

"Incoming!" Clem yelled. "Take cover."

As more explosions started erupting around them, the team scattered to find safety. Nejra dropped the loop on Mack's belt and fell to the ground. Mack swept her up into his arms and ran to the nearest house. He held her to his chest as he searched for a cellar door. He ran down the stairs with Nejra still in his arms just as the house exploded above them. Mack dropped to the ground covering Nejra's body with his own as rubble fell around them.

When the dust settled, Mack raised his head and looked around the cellar. The stairs were destroyed, but the walls were still standing. The floor above them was in ragged pieces —rays of moonlight shooting through the missing slats. He could tell the house had been flattened.

Mack pulled Nejra into a sitting position and put her back against the wall.

"Are you okay?" he said.

She nodded—her eyes wide.

"Did I hurt you when I fell on you?"

She shook her head as he sat down next to her. Mack re-inserted his radio earpiece that was dangling from its cord.

"Alpha One to Alpha Two." Mack heard Chase's voice.

"This is Alpha Two. I have Warrior with me. We're both

fine. There's no way to get out of the basement we're in. I just set off my beacon."

"We have you, Alpha Two. We're pinned down in another building. We'll get to you, but it might take a while. Our birds took out the enemy shelling position. Things should be quiet. Just sit tight."

"Roger that. Alpha Two out," Mack said as he pulled out a bottle of water.

"Do you want a drink, ma'am?" Mack held the bottle out to her. "I have plenty for both of us."

She shook her head. "Mack, if we're going to die together, please at least call me Nejra."

"We're not going to die," Mack said, brushing some of the dust off his sleeves. "They know where we are. My team will get us when it's safe. It might take a few hours though."

"A few hours," Nejra said, sighing. "What should we do with that time?"

"I'm not sure there's much we can do. Maybe take a nap."

"How can you sleep when that just happened?" She stood up and walked across the small room.

"I'm used to it," Mack said, laughing. "I can sleep pretty much anywhere."

"I thought we were going to die," she said, leaning against a wall. "I think I'm going to die most days. Ever since the war started—and my parents died—it's all I can think about sometimes. How do you get used to it?"

"I'm not sure you get used to it." Mack took his rifle from around his body and laid it next to him. "It's just more of an acceptance that it might happen."

Nejra took a deep breath. "Since the war started, all I can

think about is that I'm going to die before I've even had a chance to experience life. I'm almost desperate to do things before it's too late."

"You're going to live a long life," Mack said. "Don't be in a hurry to experience things. Most of it is overrated anyway."

"So are you saying you are not very good at sex?" she said, looking at him.

"What?" Mack jerked his head back. "How did we get there?"

"It's one of the things I want to experience before I die." Nejra held eye contact with Mack, but her voice shook. "You said we have time now."

"Wow. No," Mack said, trying to suppress a laugh. "We're not having desperation sex in this dirty building."

"I did not mean I was settling for you out of desperation. I find you very appealing," she said, pulling her shoulders back a bit. "And you can wipe that smirk off your face. There is nothing wrong with my saying that. Women are allowed to have desires, too."

"I, uh, yeah, I completely agree."

She took a small, hesitant step toward him. "So how do we go about this? Should I remove my clothes?"

"No!" Mack said, putting his hands up. "You are not having sex for the first time in this awful place. It's not happening like that."

"You don't desire me then? I have misread your intentions." She turned away from him and walked back to the opposite side of the room.

"That's not what I said. At all." Mack laid his head against the wall. "This is just not the right time. Believe me."

"I don't wish to talk about it anymore." Nejra leaned against the wall and closed her eyes. As she took a deep breath, her body started to shiver. The chilly night air had started seeping through the cracks in the ceiling. She wrapped her arms around her body to try to block the cold.

"Come over here," Mack said.

She opened her eyes to see him motioning her over to where he was sitting.

She looked at him suspiciously. "I thought you said you didn't want to have sex with me."

Mack smiled. "Again, that's not what I said. What I said is that this is not how you want your first time to be. You're way too special for that."

Nejra's lips curled into a slight smile, but her eyes narrowed as she tried to figure out Mack's intentions.

Mack patted the ground next to him. "Come here," he demanded. "Nejra, you're freezing. Please come over here."

She walked over and sat down next to him. He draped his arm over her shoulder and pulled her against his chest. Her body was tense and guarded at first, but as the warmth of Mack's body started transferring to her, she let her body melt into his.

"You're safe. I'm not going to let anything happen to you," he whispered into her hair. "Just close your eyes and try to get some sleep."

As her shallow breathing began to sync with the slow, steady rising and falling of his chest, she drifted off into the deepest sleep she had in years.

Chapter Thirteen

MILLIE, VIRGINIA BEACH, VIRGINIA, 2020

We're leaving for Rome tomorrow—me, Mason, Raine, Butch, and Hawk. We're scheduled to be there forty-eight hours, but I know timelines change. I'm panicked to leave Dad for a day, much less a week.

Mason was at the base all morning, so after I finished packing, I texted Dad to see if he wanted to go surfing. We spent a good three hours on the ocean—most of it just floating on our boards and talking. It was heavenly, but it left me so worn out. All I want to do is crash with Mason on the couch for the night.

When I walk into his house, I see a note on the kitchen island.

Check your texts. Oh yeah and one more thing, please answer your texts when I send them so I don't worry. Love you.

I haven't looked at my phone since I left to meet Dad.

Mason texted me five times. He's at the bar with the guys and wants me to join them. I don't want to go, but there's a text from Raine, too, begging me to save her from the 'testosterone explosion.'

I jump in the shower, throw on a sundress, and head out. The bar's only a half mile from the house, so I decide to walk to try to wake myself up. It doesn't work.

When I get into the bar, I see the team over at the pool tables. Mason smiles and blows me a kiss. The bartender, Pete, waves me over to him. I smile at Mason and nod toward the bar.

"Hey," Pete says. "Raine said to tell you she couldn't take it anymore. Something about testosterone. She left. You want a dirty martini?"

"No," I say, sliding onto a barstool. "I don't feel great tonight. Can I get a glass of water?"

"Yes, ma'am." He pours it and walks to the other side of the bar. I take a long drink and spin around just in time to see JJ sauntering over to me.

"Oh and here she is, the princess. You can't even let Mason have one night off, can you?" JJ rarely drinks, but I can tell he's drunk now. I don't think I've ever seen his eyes this unfocused.

"Hey JJ," I say with a forced laugh. "Is 'princess' my new nickname?"

"Oh, I imagine that nickname's been around since the day you were born," he says, way too loudly, "whether or not people called you that to your face."

I smile and take another drink of water. "You know, if you've got a problem with me, why don't you come right out and say it? We've been doing this little dance from the first day we met. It's getting old."

"You want to know what my problem is with you?" He takes a gigantic step and almost falls into me. I push my back up against the bar as he glowers down at me. "Okay, here it is. You're ruining my best friend's life. How's that? That enough of a problem for you?"

"Oh wow. Okay," I say, crossing my legs to force him to take a step back. "And how am I ruining Mason's life?"

"Well, I don't know, let's see," he says, slamming his empty beer bottle on the bar as he takes a step to the side. "How about we start with the fact that he's the best operator in the world and you forced him to quit?"

"Forced him? Damn. And here I thought you and Mase were best friends, but his best friend would know that no one makes decisions for Mason except Mason."

"That's the way it used to be." His creepy once-over of my body makes me shudder. "Then some decent pussy comes his way and all of a sudden he's whipped."

I jump off the stool and square up with him as much as I can. "You went from getting close to the line to going about a million miles beyond it. We're done."

"Yeah, go tell Mason that big, bad JJ was mean to you. Make him choose between us."

"I'm not going to tell Mason shit, because this," I say, gesturing between us, "isn't worth his time. But just so we're clear, if he ever did have to choose between us, it wouldn't end well for you because believe me, it is *way* better than decent."

I whip around and head to the bathroom. I hurry into a stall and lean against the wall. My head's spinning. For some reason, I've been dizzy a lot the last couple of weeks, but this is as intense as it's been. I feel like I'm going to pass out. I lean down with my hands on my knees and breathe in and out slowly. My head starts to clear a bit. I call Dad. He picks it up on the first ring like he always does.

"Hey, sweetie. I thought you were with Mason and the guys at the bar."

"Hey, Dad. I am, but I kind of have a headache." I take a breath to try to keep my voice from cracking. "I think I stayed up too late last night. Will you come and get me?"

"I'm out the door right now." I hear his keys jingling in the background. "Sweetie, are you okay? You have the pre-cry voice you get when you're frustrated. Are you and Mason fighting? Why isn't he bringing you home?"

"We're not fighting. I don't want to ruin his night with the guys. I'm fine. Really. Just a headache."

"Okay, I'll be there in a few minutes. Wait inside for me, okay?"

After I hang up, I splash a little cold water on my face and head out to tell Mason I'm leaving. I see him scanning the bar anxiously. His eyes land on me as I walk from behind the bar. He hustles over to me.

"Hey," he says, putting his arm around me. "Where were you? Are you okay?"

"Yeah, but I have a headache. I'm going home."

"Aww, baby." His fingers start massaging my temples. "We can go home. Let me tell the guys I'm leaving."

"No, Mase. Dad's coming to get me—"

I barely get it out when Dad comes charging through the

door. He looks pissed. Mason looks from me to him and then back at me.

"Millie, what's wrong? What happened?" Mason gets on my eye level. He's figured out that if he stares directly into my eyes from only a few inches out that I will confess all of my secrets to him. I hate that he's figured that out.

"I was about to ask the same question," Dad says, pulling me back from Mason. "Did you say something to upset my daughter?"

"Dad, no, I told you it wasn't him."

"What do you mean it wasn't me?" Mason looks around the room like he's about to take a rifle out and start firing. "Who was it?"

"Nobody." My voice cracks.

Mason grabs my shoulders. I try to wriggle away as he gets down in my face again. "You sound like you're going to cry. Why are you frustrated? Who said something to you?"

"C'mon, Mason," Dad says, spitting out the words. "If it wasn't you, you know it was that asshole JJ."

"Dad!" I spin around to look at him.

"What?" Mason releases me and turns around to find JJ. "Was it JJ? What did he say?"

"Nothing. Mase, it's fine." I turn to Dad. "Can we just go home, please?"

Dad pulls me to him as Mason charges toward JJ.

"What the fuck did you say to her?" Mason says, pushing JJ back a few steps.

JJ laughs as he takes a slow drink of his beer. "Just the truth, brother."

"Stay here, Millie," Dad says as he takes three enormous

steps, quickly covering the distance between him and JJ. "I think I warned you last night to stay away from my daughter. Do you have a learning problem?"

"Why don't you take your daughter and go back to wherever you came from?" JJ takes a step toward Dad.

Mason catches him mid-stride and shoves him roughly against the wall and then spins around to block Dad's advance.

"Mack, please go home," he says, holding his hands in the air, making sure not to touch Dad. "Please get Millie out of here. I'll take care of this."

Dad nods a few times and then takes a step backward—his eyes still locked on JJ. "Take care of him, Mason," he growls. "Or I'm coming back here to do it for you."

"I'll take care of it," Mason says, looking from Dad to me. "Babe, go home with your Dad. I'll be there in a few minutes."

"Mase, don't get in a fight over this," I say, resting my hands on his chest. His body temperature is so hot. It feels like it's going to burn a hole in his T-shirt. "Please. You said yourself JJ's just stressed because he's the new team lead. It's no big deal. I'm fine. Don't get in a fight."

He hugs me and then turns me around toward the door. "I'm fine, baby. Just go home, okay?"

I look up at him. He's trying to make his eyes look gentle as he smiles at me, but they're hard and cold.

"Mase—"

"I'll see you in a little bit." He kisses me on the top of the head and pushes me gently toward the door.

Dad grabs my hand and pulls me the rest of the way out.

"Dad," I say, trying to turn around and go back into the bar.

"He'll be fine, sweetie. It's a guy thing. Let them work it out." He puts his arm around me and pulls me to the car. "Now, do you want to tell me what JJ said to you?"

"Nope," I say, "not even a little bit."

He shakes his head and smiles. "You're still doing it."

"Doing what?"

"Holding back information from people because you think you know better than they do what's best for them."

"I don't do that," I say, looking down.

"You've been doing that since you were a little kid. You don't want to be responsible for someone getting hurt, so you hold back anything you think might get them too involved."

I tilt my head—my eyebrows raising. "I wonder who taught me how to do that?"

He laughs and kisses my forehead. "Yeah, I guess I wasn't a very good role model, huh?"

"No, you weren't very good," I say as I hug him. "You were the best."

Chapter Fourteen

MASON, VIRGINIA BEACH, VIRGINIA, 2020

After I watch Millie and Mack walk out the door, I spin around and charge at JJ.

"Man, what the fuck is your problem?" I say, shoving him up against the wall. "If you come at her again, I will kill you."

He doesn't try to fight back. He just stares at me. "So that's your choice, huh?"

"Are you asking me to choose between you and Millie?" I take a few steps back, shaking my head slowly. "Because if you are, it's her, hands down. It's her before anyone. It's her before anything. Not even close."

He pushes himself off the wall. "I guess that's it then. Fifteen years of friendship gone because of some girl."

"You know damn well she's not 'some girl.' I'm in love with her. I'm going to spend the rest of my life with her. If you end our friendship because of that, that's on you, not me."

"Why don't you go home to her then?" he says, bumping my shoulder as he walks by me. "Echo Team's got some things to talk about. I guess that doesn't involve you anymore."

"I'm going home to her as soon as possible, but I've got something I need to talk to you about first. I asked Culver to let me be the one to tell you."

He turns around. "What? Did you have him pull me off as team lead? I say something bad about your girlfriend and you try to take down my career?"

"I'm the one who fucking got you the job, asshole? Culver didn't think you were ready to lead. I talked him into it."

I regret saying it instantly. He looks like someone just shot him right in the face.

He takes a step back over to me. "What are you talking about?"

"I'm not talking about anything." I run my hands roughly over my face. "I told you, you're going to be a great team leader."

"But Culver doesn't want me there? Is that what you're saying?" His voice shakes with anger. "You had to beg him to take me?"

I put my hand on his shoulder. He shoves it off. "I didn't beg him, Jay. He just wasn't sure. He probably wasn't sure of me at first either. It's no big deal."

He laughs. "You know damn well no one ever questioned the great Mason Davis. They've been rolling out the red carpet for you since the day you entered the program. So, is that what you want to tell me—that Culver isn't sure of me? Message received. Thanks for that, best friend."

I take a deep breath. "That's not what I wanted to tell you. The CIA director wants Millie and me for a special assignment. We're leaving tomorrow. We're taking Butch, Hawk, and Raine with us. You're going to have to get mission-ready with some new guys and a new agent. I know it puts you a few days behind. I'm sorry it's going to jam you up, but it's happening."

"Un-fucking-believable." He looks down and exhales a long breath. "I thought you had my back, but you're trying everything you can to sink me."

"That's not what this is, man."

"That's exactly what it is—everything for her. Just leave. Go back to her. You're not doing anyone any good here."

I nod and look at him for a few more seconds before I slowly turn around.

"She must have some really sweet pussy—"

The words are barely out of his mouth before I send him to the ground with a hard right hook. I jump on top of him and land a few more punches before Hawk and Ty pull me off.

"Don't you ever talk about her again!" I yell as I wrestle to get free. I've almost broken away from them when Butch and Bryce step in front of me. The four of them start pushing me toward the door. I'm pointing at JJ. "You don't look at her! You don't talk to her! You don't even fucking think about her!"

They manage to get me out the door. Hawk and Butch pin me against the wall with Ty and Bryce at the ready as reinforcements.

"Go home, Mase," Butch says. "You've got to go home right now. Just walk away. It's not worth it."

"We'll see you tomorrow, brother," Hawk says, trying to

guide me toward my car. "Let's get to Rome and forget about all this over a bunch of Peronis."

My eyes are still focused on the bar's door, but I'm starting to nod. I know they're right. I want to kill JJ right now, but it's not worth it. I stop resisting and walk to my car. I nod at them as I get in.

It takes me about two of the usual ten minutes to drive from the bar to my house. I want to see Millie so badly right now. When I pull into the driveway, Mack's sitting on my front porch. Millie's nowhere to be seen.

"You put him down?" Mack says as I get out of the car.

"He's down," I snarl. "He's not coming back at her."

"She told me he's your best friend. I get that, but if you can't take care of him, I will."

"Mack, I told you I took care of it," I say, glaring at him. I want to punch him right now, too. "It's done."

"You said that last night at the barbecue, but here he is tonight, coming at her again—"

"Mack!" I take a long breath and force myself to calm down. "Look, man, I told Millie a while back that I loved her with everything in me, but that I still had no problem believing that it's only half as much as you love her. I still believe that. I know she's your everything—and I'm fine with that—but you've got to give me some room to love her, too. You've got to back off a little."

He stares at me for a good two minutes without moving. He finally stands up and walks out toward his car.

"You're right," he says, turning around. "I'll back off. I know you love her. I appreciate the way you take care of her."

"Thank you," I say, walking over to him and extending my

hand. He shakes it. "I'll never let anything bad happen to your daughter. You know that."

"Yeah, I do."

As he turns around, I say, "Will you repeat that first part you said? That part about me being, uh, what was it? I think it rhymes with light."

He shakes his head. "We're having a nice moment and you have to go and ruin it."

"Since that's probably the only time you're ever going to tell me I'm right, I thought I'd try to hear it again," I say, smiling.

He growls at me. "She wants me to come over tomorrow morning to say goodbye to her before you leave. You have a problem with that?"

"She won't leave unless she gets to hug you again, so yeah, you're going to need to be here."

He nods and starts laughing. "Did you really ask her to marry you?"

"Yeah—"

"Aww, man, rookie mistake. It's way too early." He smiles as he gets into the car. He rolls down the window. "Did she flat out say no or did she say she'd think about it?"

"See you tomorrow, Mack."

He's still laughing as I turn around to go into the house. Millie's sleeping on the couch under her usual mound of blankets. I lift her into my arms to carry her back to the bedroom.

"Mase," she says, looking up at me with sleepy eyes. "Is everything okay?"

"Yeah, baby." I kiss the top of her head as I lay her down on the bed and cover her back up.

"Are you and JJ okay?" she says, sitting up.

"Everything's fine." I try to get her to lie back down, but she climbs into my lap. "Mills, try to go back to sleep, okay? We have an early call tomorrow."

"You don't have to choose between us, not for me. You know that, right?" Her eyes are insistent.

"I know, baby, and I appreciate that, but it's always you— before family, friends, work, whatever—it's you."

"But—"

"Millie," I say, kissing her. "I understand what you're saying. Thank you, but that makes me know even more that you're always the right decision. Now, will you please go back to sleep?"

She starts nibbling on my ear.

"Baby, we have to get up so early. You need sleep."

"You know I always sleep better after a workout," she whispers right into my ear. She knows that turns me on.

"Millicent," I say sternly. "Stop."

"What?" She lowers her head and looks at me—her green eyes sparkling under her long eyelashes.

"Stop looking at me like that," I say, shaking my head, but we both know it's too late. She can feel how hard I am.

"Like what?" Her hands crawl underneath my T-shirt.

I flip her over and flatten her to the bed. "You know very well what look I'm talking about. The look that makes me want to never let you out of this bed."

"I'd be okay with that—"

I growl as my mouth covers hers. My hand quickly goes between her legs. She's ready for me, but I try to hold back a little. Although unlike every girl I've ever been with, she's never needed much foreplay. In fact, she gets a little demanding when I try to slow her down. She lets me finger her for a few minutes, but then she starts impatiently arching her back.

"Inside," she whines as she takes me in her hand.

God, that whiny, little purr she has. I could bust just hearing it. "Okay, baby."

When I slide into her, she wraps her legs around my waist and pulls the rest of me into her. She buries her face in my neck. As I start pumping harder, she bites my shoulder—like she does when she's ready to cum. The feeling of her teeth on my skin always sends me over the edge. Her body shakes as she lets out a series of low moans. That sound. God, I'd do anything to hear that sound for the rest of my life.

"It's always you, baby," I whisper. "You over everything."

I take a few more pumps and let go—depositing what feels like every last bit of me into her. She lets out one last long moan.

"Fuck," I say as I collapse on top of her. "That keeps getting better every time we do it."

She giggles underneath me. "Let's try it again just to make sure."

I roll over and pull her onto my chest. "I'm denying you more until you get a good night's rest."

"So rude—"

"You promised you'd go to sleep after, baby. You've been so tired lately. Get some sleep, okay?"

"Okay," she sighs as she rolls off me and buries her face in my pillow. She always steals my pillow. It's adorable.

I rub her back until she slips back into sleep. After I finish packing for Rome, I crawl into bed and pull her into a spoon. She makes a little whimpering noise as she wiggles her body into mine. I catch my breath. I still haven't gotten used to how good it feels when she snuggles into me.

So many people questioned my decision to leave active duty, but when I'm next to her—with her body against mine—I know I made the right choice. If this is what the rest of my life looks like, I'm the luckiest man on earth.

Chapter Fifteen

SARAJEVO, BOSNIA, 1994

After the team got back from the mountains, the agency switched them to another base location. Since someone apparently leaked information on their raid, George had cut his already skeleton staff to himself, Nejra, and the SEAL team. They took over a house abandoned by one of the opposition leaders. It was secluded, gated, and even had a security system.

"They knew we were coming tonight," George said. "Until we figure out how, we're going to stay put. We'll be here at least a few days—maybe a week. Get comfortable. There's a gym in the basement. Feel free to use it. If you go outside, try to stay under the covered patio. No one should be able to see us through the trees."

"All we want to do now is sleep," Harry said. "Where's our bunk room?"

"This house is huge," George said. "There are enough rooms for each of you to have your own."

"Damn, maybe I can get some real sleep if I don't have to listen to Harry's ass snoring all night," Clem said. He quickly turned to Nejra. "Ma'am, I'm sorry for my language. It's a bad habit."

Nejra smiled. "It must be lost in translation, but Harry is a unique man if he can snore out of his bottom."

"Yeah, he's unique for sure," Chase said, shaking his head. "Are all the rooms upstairs?"

George nodded. "Nejra and I will grab rooms on this level and there's one more down here. The rest are upstairs."

Nejra walked toward the room George pointed out for her. She lingered outside the door to try to figure out where Mack was sleeping.

"Do you want the room on this level?" Mack said to Chase.

"Naw, man, I better be on the second level," Chase said as he walked toward the stairs. "You know we want the best shooters on the high ground and that ain't you, brother."

Mack turned around to find Nejra peeking at him over her shoulder. She looked away and ducked into her bedroom. He sighed as he walked down the hall to his room. He already knew she was going to be trouble, but he wasn't sure what he could do about it. And he wasn't sure he wanted to do anything about it.

He was attracted to her—very attracted to her. She was beautiful, but it was more than that. She was smart and funny —two qualities he never found in the women who flocked around him back home. It worried him, though. She was sweet and vulnerable. He knew he would probably never see her again after they left. He decided he wouldn't pursue her, but he was almost sure she'd show up at his room at some point in the next few days.

Mack was in bed, staring at the ceiling like he did most nights. He didn't sleep very long when they were away on missions— maybe an hour here and there if he was lucky. This job had a way of getting in his head.

He was about to fade off to sleep when he heard a faint knock at his door. He sprang up and grabbed his pistol off the table. He walked across the room. Just as he got to the door, he heard a hushed voice.

"It's Nejra."

He took a deep breath as he looked up at the ceiling, shaking his head. He knew he didn't have the willpower to turn her away. When he opened the door, she shifted nervously as she looked up at him, but her eyes were determined. He opened the door wider and reached for her hand. She raised it and let him guide her into the room.

Mack closed the door and pulled her into a hug. "Are you sure?" he whispered. "You don't have to do this. You'll have plenty of time in your life—"

She pushed him back and looked up at him. "I've never been more sure of anything in my life."

He took another deep breath as he searched her eyes for any sign of hesitation. He couldn't find any. He hugged her again to give her time to change her mind. She raised on tiptoe and opened her lips slightly. When he kissed her, he could tell she had never even kissed anyone before.

He let her go and looked into her eyes again. "How old are you?"

"I'm twenty-four," she said, frowning. "I am more than old enough. My mother was married when she was seventeen."

"We're not married," Mack said, walking over to sit on the side of the bed. "Why don't you wait? Maybe you should be married first."

"Were you married for your first time?" Nejra pulled her shoulders back.

"It's different—"

"It's not different," she said, crossing her arms. "How old are you?"

"Twenty-two."

"Then I am older than you. I should have some control over this situation."

Mack smiled. "You have all the control over this situation, every bit of it. We're only going to do what you want to do."

"If that were true, we would already be doing it," she said, walking over to him and trying to kiss him again.

"Nejra, sit down." Mack patted the bed next to him. "We're going to talk first."

"Is this part of how you do sex?" she asked as she plopped down next to him.

"No, it's not part of how I do sex," he said, smiling, "but it's going to be part of how I do sex with you."

Mack pushed himself back against the wall and reached out to pull Nejra between his legs with her back resting on his chest. She relaxed against him, pulling his arms around her. He leaned his head down and kissed her cheek, letting his lips linger a bit.

"You're a virgin?" he whispered.

"Yes."

"And what happens down the road when you want to get married? Your husband's going to know—"

"Then he will have to accept it or he can find someone else to marry."

Mack laughed softly to himself. She definitely wasn't scared of him or any other man.

"You say what you're thinking, don't you?"

"I always have. My mother told me men didn't find that attractive." She looked up at him. "Is that true?"

"I can't speak for all men, but it's not true for me." He kissed her lips lightly. "I like a woman who knows what she wants."

Nejra turned her body around to face him. "Prove it," she whispered.

Mack smiled as he pulled her onto his lap, pushing her legs wide so she was straddling him.

"Yes, ma'am," he said as he weaved his hands through her long hair and pulled her in for a deep kiss.

Chapter Sixteen

For the first time since I found Dad, I'm about to go for more than twelve hours without seeing him. It's all I've been able to think about this morning and it has me frazzled. I'm usually organized and focused on travel days, but Mason's had to push me all morning. It doesn't help that I ate a two-day-old burrito for breakfast and promptly threw it up. I didn't have time to eat anything else, so now I'm having a low-blood-sugar breakdown.

"Damn it," I say as I rummage through my backpack. "I forgot to pack food."

We're in a conference room at the base waiting for the agency's private plane to arrive. Dad and Chase are here to see us off. I look up to see Mason and Dad pulling food out of their packs. Mason hands me my favorite protein bar. Dad has fruit roll-ups—my go-to snack when I was a kid. They look at each other and then back at me.

"Here, sweetie," Dad says, reaching his arm beyond Mason's. "They're strawberry—your favorite."

Mason rolls his eyes, leaning his head back a bit to make sure Dad doesn't see him. I grab both snacks. They settle back in their seats uncomfortably, taking another look at each other.

"The fact you're both carrying snacks for me is maybe the best thing that's ever happened in my life," I say, trying not to laugh as I look at their stern faces. "So if you have some male, territorial thing going on, work it out on your own time."

They put their heads back against the wall and close their eyes. Their legs kick out in front of them in unison as their big arms cross defensively over their chests. I wonder if they're ever going to figure out how similar they are—bullheaded, fierce, and just tender to the core.

Chase taps me on the leg. I look down to see him passing me a bag of almonds.

"For when you crash from all the sugar they gave you," he whispers.

As I open the almonds, I look over to Butch and Hawk. Butch is staring at me.

"You're the most spoiled person I've ever met," he says, gnawing on his ever-present toothpick. "It's like they're offering gifts to their queen."

"As it should be," I say, throwing an almond at him. "What did you bring your queen?"

"I'm happy to give you a good smack on the behind. That's what you need the most," he says, throwing the almond back at me. "But since I don't have the energy for that right now, why don't you hook me up with some of those fruit roll-ups? Strawberry's my favorite, too."

I toss him a bag as Raine walks into the room. "The plane just landed," she says. "They're ready for us."

Dad's eyes pop open as he reaches out to take my hand. He knows I'm struggling about leaving him.

"C'mon, sweetie," he says, smiling. "I'll walk you out."

Raine, Butch, and Hawk board the plane, but Mason lags back to wait for me while I say goodbye to Dad. He probably thinks he's going to have to drag me onto the plane. He might be right.

"I'm going to be here when you get back, Mills," Dad says as he hugs me a little tighter.

"I know."

"Do you?" He pushes me back to look into my glassy eyes. "I'm going to be here. Just make sure you get back safely."

I nod, looking down.

"Mason, come over here," Dad says, waving him over to us. "I need a witness."

Mason walks up and frowns when he sees my teary eyes.

Dad tilts my chin up. "Millie, I need you to make me a promise."

"Anything," I say, looking up at him.

"From this moment until you get back here, promise me you won't go anywhere—and I mean anywhere—without Mason."

I take a deep breath and nod my head.

"Use your words, sweetie." Dad obviously remembers when I was little, I thought if I didn't say something out loud, I didn't have to follow through on it.

"I promise," I say, rolling my eyes at him.

"The entire sentence, please," Dad says, smiling. God, he knows me so well.

"I promise I won't go anywhere without Mason from right now until we get back here."

"Very good," he says, kissing my forehead.

"Damn. Nice work, Mack," Mason says, laughing. "She would never make me that promise."

"Mase, you might want to remember who you're in the relationship with—"

"It's been clear from the beginning that this was going to be a package deal."

"Hmm," I say, squinting as I look back and forth between them. "Maybe we should go back to you two not liking each other."

"Too late, babe. Mack loves me now," Mason smiles as he backs up a little bit to give me one last second alone with Dad. Dad hugs me again.

"Are you still going down to the Outer Banks tomorrow?" I say, not lifting my head from his chest.

"Yeah. Chase and Mar are coming with me."

"Are you going to see Carol?"

He sighs. "Yeah, she agreed to have coffee with me, but she's pissed that I disappeared without telling her, so we'll see where it leads us—if anywhere."

I look up at him. "Are you in love with her, Dad?"

He takes a deep breath and slowly nods.

"Use your words, please."

He bursts out laughing—the sound vibrating in his chest. It's the first time I've heard his unbridled laugh since he's been back. "Yeah, Mills. I think I might be. Is that okay?"

"It's perfect."

He smiles. "Get on the plane. Text me when you land."

"Okay, let me know how it goes with Carol."

Mason walks back over to us and laces his fingers into mine.

"Bring her home, Mason," Dad says as Mason pulls me toward the plane.

Mason looks back at Dad. "I'll make sure she always gets back to you, Mack. For the rest of my life. I promise."

Chapter Seventeen

MASON, IN-FLIGHT, VIRGINIA BEACH TO ROME, 2020

"Well, this is a little different than we're used to," I say as we walk into the private jet.

Plush seats surround a table loaded with snacks and drinks. A big-screen television hangs from the wall with an enormous vase of fresh flowers underneath it. Butch and Hawk are already fully reclined in the captain's chairs at the front of the cabin—eyes closed, arms folded over their chests. Raine kicked off her shoes and is stretched out on one of the couches. I pull Millie over to the couch opposite her.

"It's one of the director's private planes," Raine says as she sips on a flute of orange juice. "Not too many people get to use them. I swear, Millie, I think he might be in love with you."

"Is that right?" I say, smiling as I tilt Millie's chin up to look at me.

"You don't need to worry about me leaving you for Paul Ward," she says. "I might leave you for Butch—"

"I heard that." Butch peeks at us through his one open eye. "And frankly, Mills, it's about time you realized who the real catch is here."

I swing my legs up on the couch and pull Millie down between them—her back resting against my chest. She sits up straight—looking back at me uncomfortably.

"Wait, Mase, this is a business trip," she says, trying to scoot to the other side of the couch.

I wrap my arms around her waist and pull her back. "It's not like everyone on this plane doesn't know we're together."

She still won't relax back into me. She looks at Raine. "Is this weird? It's weird, right?"

"I mean, I think we'd all appreciate if you didn't make out—"

"Really appreciate," Hawk says with his eyes still closed.

"But if you want to sit by each other," Raine continues, "I don't think anyone cares. Right, Butch?"

"Well, I mean if Mason's not going to snuggle me, then he might as well snuggle Millie," he says, opening his eyes slightly. "Raine, bring me some orange juice."

"What am I? A flight attendant? You've got legs." Raine leans back against the pillows on her couch and pops open her laptop.

Millie finally rests back into my chest. I give her a discreet kiss on the top of her head.

"Okay, I think we're all getting a little too comfortable," Millie says. "Raine, why don't you get us up to date on what's happening on the ground?"

Butch and Hawk open their eyes but don't make any effort to sit up.

"Yep," Raine says, putting her orange juice down and turning her computer screen to us. "Well, first, they haven't located Amar Petrovic. He's still missing. We found the cab that picked him up outside their flat the morning he disappeared. The cab log shows he was dropped off outside the port at Civitavecchia. Of course, that was three days ago so he could be anywhere by now. The police are looking for the cab driver. They should have questioned him by the time we arrive. Amar's wife, Amila, still hasn't talked to anyone. She insists on waiting for Millie. Their three kids are spread out through Europe. We have people watching them in case Amar shows up."

"This is the guy we grabbed in Sarajevo on our first mission with you, right?" Hawk says. Raine pulls up a picture of Amar and holds it up for everyone to see.

"Yeah, you brought him back to the embassy for me to interview," Millie says. "He led us to Haroun Hadzic who was hiding up in the mountains—that night we got in a firefight."

"I remember," Hawk says. "So at the time, you didn't think Petrovic was involved in the network, right? He'd been living in Spain for twenty years or so, but now you think he was running the ground game for Sayid Custovic?"

"I don't think that at all. The agency does." Millie hesitates. "Look, full disclosure, Amar was friends with my mom. He's the one who called my dad to tell him to get me out of Bosnia when I was a baby. And then, he contacted Dad again when Yusef Hadzic was trying to find me when I was a teenager. That's why Dad disappeared. So my past with Amar is more than a little complicated. I've only talked to him that one time in Sarajevo, but I didn't get the vibe that he was involved in my uncle's network at all. I don't peg him for this."

"But there was someone coordinating for them on the ground, right? A civilian?" Butch says.

"Yeah, apparently." Raine flips through a few documents on her computer. "Our analysts are still going through Sayid's journals. He recorded everything. He refers to someone as "Mir." That's the person who seemed to be coordinating efforts for them on the ground."

"Does Mir mean anything to you, Millie?" I ask.

"I guess it could be an abbreviation for a name: Mira, Miranda," she says, shrugging her shoulders. "And it means "peace" in Bosnian. Other than that, your guess is as good as mine."

"But the agency thinks Petrovic is "Mir"?" Hawks asks.

"Yeah," Millie says. "They were closing in on him when he disappeared, so they think he's running."

"If you don't think he's the guy, why do you think he's running?" Butch says.

"That, I don't know. And he might not even be running from us or running at all," Mille says. "His wife might know. That's the reason I'm going over because she says she'll only talk to me."

"Why do you think she'll only talk to you?" I say.

"Who knows? She told the agents on the ground that she knows me, but we barely met in Sarajevo. Maybe she's just intimidated and thinks I can help her in some way. Or maybe Amar told her to ask for me before he disappeared. I guess we'll find out."

"So, are we here to protect you?" Hawk says to Millie.

"No, you're here to grab Amar if we locate him—"

"We can do both," I say as I tighten my arms around her.

After Raine briefs us on a few more details, everyone settles in to get some sleep before we land. I grab a few blankets out of an overhead compartment and put them over Millie. She's already sound asleep on the couch. I hesitate as I start to crawl in behind her. I look back at Raine who's still working on her computer.

"No one cares, Mase. Seriously," she says, smiling. "It's just the five of us. We're family."

I nod as I curl up behind Millie and spoon her to me. She wriggles back into me as usual. This might be the best assignment I've had in my entire career. I could get used to it.

Chapter Eighteen

SARAJEVO, BOSNIA, 1994

"I would like to do that again," Nejra said as she lifted her head from Mack's chest and nudged his mouth onto hers for another kiss.

Mack kissed her softly. "Yes, I would like to do that again, too," he said, smiling.

She looked down his body. "It does not seem ready. Do I need to do something to encourage it?"

Mack's deep laugh rebounded off the walls of the room. "Believe me, you're doing enough just lying naked on my chest. Give me a minute to recover."

"It needs to rest between times?" She put her head back down on his chest.

"Yeah, baby, it does," he said as he stroked her hair. "Did your mom not tell you anything about sex?'

"Nothing, literally not one word. It's not something we discuss until the day of a woman's wedding and even then it's not nearly enough information. My Aunt Aza told me a few things. She said it might hurt the first time, but that was not my experience."

Mack kissed the top of her head. "I'm glad. I wanted your first time to be good."

"Are you supposed to feel like your entire body is exploding?'

"If you're doing it right—"

"And does it hurt for you? You made a loud noise—"

Mack smiled, pulling her chin up to look at him. "That wasn't a painful noise. Believe me."

She looked satisfied. "Then I did it right."

"You did it very right," he said, pulling a blanket up to cover them. "I'm still worried about when you get married. They'll expect you to be a virgin, right?"

"Honestly, I'm not even sure I ever want to get married."

"Why not?"

"I don't know how marriage is for you, but in my culture, it can be very repressive. The husband has too much control over what his wife does with her life. I don't want anyone telling me what I can and cannot do."

"You just need to find the right person," Mack said. "Someone who will encourage you to do whatever you want and be there to protect you while you're doing it."

Nejra sighed. "I don't think that type of man exists in my world."

"Then get out of this world. Move to the United States. You would have more freedom there."

"Just like that? Leave everything I know behind?"

"You could—"

"No, I couldn't." She snuggled into the crook of his neck

as he tightened his arm around her. "I can't leave my brother. After our parents died, I was the only reason he even got up in the morning. He acts like he's tough but down deep, he has a sensitive soul. He would fall apart if I left."

"If you change your mind, I'll help you get to the U.S. I'll give you my address before I leave. Do you promise you'll contact me if you ever want to move—if you ever need anything at all?"

"I promise," she said as he pulled her on top of him.

He kissed her deeply as he took her hand and moved it down his body.

"It seems to be working again," she said, giggling.

"Yes, it does. But if you make that sexy, little sound again, it's not going to be working much longer," he laughed as he flipped her over, his hands moving quickly down her body.

Mack's team stayed in Sarajevo for a week but didn't see any more action. Every day, Mack would hang out with the team, and every night, Nejra would visit his room. She would stay with him most of the night—talking, snuggling, sleeping, and making love. He looked so forward to her visits that he almost felt physically sick when Chase told him they were leaving the next morning.

"What? We haven't even done anything here," Mack said. "Can they not get a read on the HVTs?"

"That's not the problem," Chase said. "The higher-ups have decided on another approach. I'm not sure why. You know how it is: a bunch of hurry-up-and-wait."

"So we're wheels up in the morning?" Mack said, trying to keep the anger he was feeling out of his voice.

"Yeah," Chase said, locking eyes with him. "You might want to wrap up any loose ends here tonight."

Mack stared back at him. "I don't have any loose ends here."

Chase patted his shoulder as he walked away. "Your room's right below mine, brother. Wheels up at seven hundred."

Mack went to Nejra's room and knocked lightly on the door. When she opened the door, he took her hand and pulled her down the hall to his room.

"We're leaving tomorrow," he said as he closed the door. "I don't think we'll be back."

She nodded, looking at him directly in the eyes. "I knew this time was coming. I don't want you to leave, but I'm prepared. There is no need for you to feel an ounce of guilt."

He hugged her. "I don't feel guilty, but I'm going to miss you. I enjoyed our time together."

"Yes," she said, snuggling into his chest. "You were the perfect first partner."

He pushed her back a little to look at her. "Nejra, I enjoyed the sex—no doubt—but I liked getting to know you. You're smart, sweet, funny. I'm going to miss talking to you."

"Do you suppose we will ever see each other again?"

"I don't know," he said, smiling down at her. "Will you reconsider coming to the U.S.?"

She shook her head. "Not right now. Maybe one day."

"Okay," he said, walking over to the nightstand. "This is my address. We're not supposed to share this with anyone for security reasons. I can't give you my phone number because of the tracker system in my phone, but I need you to be able to reach me. Will you please write to me and let me know you're safe?"

"I will write to you."

"And if you ever want to leave here and come to the U.S., I'll figure out a way to make it work. Please promise me you'll write me."

"I promise," she said as she tilted her head up to him. "Will you make love to me one more time?"

He nodded as he leaned down to kiss her. "I wish I could make love to you forever. You're beautiful, Nejra, in every single way possible."

Chapter Nineteen

MILLIE, ROME, ITALY, 2020

When we land in Rome, one of our agents meets us at a private airport. He has a Mercedes Sprinter waiting for us. As we walk over to him, his eyes light up as he looks at Raine and me. I don't think I've seen him before, but his large grin indicates he thinks he knows us.

"Welcome to Rome," he says. "Damn, you get to fly over on the director's plane? Which one of you is fucking him?"

Mason, Butch, and Hawk take quick steps toward him. Hawk gets there first and grabs him by the collar. "What did you say to them?"

"Hawk, it's fine," Raine says, getting in between them. "This is Brad Simmons. He's our ground contact here. And he's been an asshole since the first day I met him."

"Nice to see you again, too, Raine," he says, smiling and opening his arms for a hug. Raine declines. "And Millie Marsh, I haven't seen you since our training days back at Langley."

"Yeah," I say. "That long ago, huh?"

"You don't remember me, do you?" he says, shaking his head. "I guess it's true what they say: The hotter the girl, the bigger the bitch."

Hawk has barely released Brad when Mason throws him against the van. I knew it was coming, but I didn't even try to stop him. Honestly, I think it might do Brad some good.

"How about—for the rest of this trip—you shut the fuck up and just do your job?" Mason says, leaning his forearm into Brad's neck. He pushes him one more time before he releases him.

Brad coughs a few times, trying to recover. "Well, I'm guessing that one's your boyfriend," he says, under his breath.

"Nope, this one is," I say, putting my arm around Butch.

"Mills, you keep saying stuff like that," Butch says, winking at me, "I'm going to start to take you seriously."

"It's about time," I say, kissing the side of his head before I look back at Brad. "Where are we headed?"

Brad looks from Mason to Butch and then back at me. "The director has you staying at one of our houses over in Aventino—not too far from the Colosseum, but we're going to the Petrovics' house first. The wife, Amina, has been waiting to talk to you. I don't think she's much of a threat, but these guys should be strapped just in case."

Brad opens the back of the van and unlocks a cabinet to reveal a stash of guns and ammo. The guys walk over and start gearing up.

"You like me better now, don't you?" Brad says, looking from Mason to the weapons.

"No," Mason says, glaring at him. Brad takes a quick step back when Mason grabs a rifle.

"Mase, c'mon," I say, walking over next to him. "We're in Rome, not Jalalabad. Don't you think your sidearms will be enough? We don't want to scare the poor woman."

He looks at me sternly but puts the rifle back in the cabinet before grabbing a few more mags for his pistol. Hawk and Butch do the same.

"Let's get going," Mason growls. "This entire op is giving me bad vibes for some reason."

As we start loading into the back of the van, Brad holds out his hand to help Raine.

"You're in the front with the driver," Mason says, blocking Brad's hand and helping Raine in himself. "And if you try to touch either of them again, we're going to have a problem."

Brad turns around quickly and heads to the front. We drive through the busy streets of Rome for about thirty minutes before we pull up at a luxury apartment building near the Piazza di Spagna—by the Spanish Steps. It seems like a pretty high-rent neighborhood for a dentist.

"She asked to talk to you alone," Brad says to me as we get out. He eyes Mason nervously. "Elevator to the penthouse. They have the entire floor."

"Hawk, stay down here with Raine—and him," Mason says, motioning toward Brad. "Butch, on me. Mills, we're coming into the apartment with you, but we'll give you some space."

"That's fine," I say, nodding. I seriously don't care that much. I'm not sure why Amina wants to talk to me, but I can't imagine it's going to be that enlightening.

When the elevator opens, Amina Petrovic is waiting for us. I vaguely remember meeting her in Sarajevo. That night, she looked disheveled and scared as we prepared to move them quickly to Portugal to get them off Sayid's radar. Today, she's the picture of luxury. She's wearing a neatly pressed white linen dress—perfect for the hot summer day. Her dark hair is pulled off her face in a loose chignon. She has on full makeup and as I step toward her, I can smell her light, citrusy perfume. She seems a little too put together for a woman with a missing husband.

She extends her hand to me—several diamond tennis bracelets glittering from her wrist. "Millie, it's a pleasure to see you again."

"It's my pleasure," I say, smiling as I shake her hand. "I wish it were under better circumstances."

"Yes," she says as she looks at Mason and Butch. "I see you're traveling with protection. I don't know that they'll be needed in Rome."

"They adapt well to every situation." I motion toward the sitting area. "Shall we talk?"

"Right to business," she says, smiling. "Your grandma was like that. She was never one for wasting time. Let's speak in Bosnian so we can have a little more privacy?"

"Of course," I say, switching to Bosnian. "You knew my family?"

"Very well. We lived in the same neighborhood. Your mother and I attended the same school. She was two years older than me." She pauses for a second and then smiles. "My husband was in love with her."

She's trying to look amused, but I can see the anger deep

in her eyes. That must be a sore spot. It seems like a good place to start. "Really? Amar didn't tell me that."

"Yes, because she rejected him." Her tone is even, but a little bitter. "It was always a sensitive subject for him."

"I'm sure he was delighted when you came along," I say, smiling broadly, "so he could forget all about my mother."

She laughs loudly. "My husband never forgot about your mother."

"Well, I suppose when someone dies that young, they become immortalized, don't they?" I reach out and touch her hand. I'm trying not to lay it on too thick, but I can tell she's feeling a little uncomfortable. I need to give her some power back. "I'm sure my mom wouldn't have made Amar nearly as good a wife as you've been to him over the years."

"No, but not because she wasn't a lovely person. She was," she says, hesitating. "She just never felt the same way for Amar that he did for her."

I smile and nod like a good therapist. She seems like she wants to say more. She looks at me for a few seconds and then continues, "I spent some time with your mom in our teenage years, but I'll admit, I was using her to be closer to her brother, Sayid. I believe you met him—at the end."

"I did," I say. "I'm sure he was a much different person when you knew him."

"Much different!" Her entire face lights up. "He was quiet and kind, and very smart. Our parents matched us up early in our lives, but I'm afraid that never came to pass after your mother died. Sayid was barely hanging on when your grandparents died. Nejra's death sent him over the edge."

"Did you lose touch with him after he left for Pakistan?" I

already know she didn't. Everything about her face is telling me the truth.

"Yes, I'm afraid I never talked to him again after he left for Pakistan. And then I'm sure you know, he disappeared up into the mountains with Yusef Hadzic. I believe you met him, too."

"I did," I say, switching back to English. "Amina is a lovely name. Is it Arabic?"

"It is," she says, switching back with me. "I was named after my great-grandmother. What origin is Millie?"

"My full name is Millicent. I believe it's French. I'm not sure why my dad named me that. It means "brave strength." Maybe he was trying to project its meaning onto my life."

"It seems that he succeeded," she says, smiling tightly. She's done with the small talk.

"What does Amina mean in Arabic?"

"Is that not one of the many languages you speak?" Her tone is getting more bitter.

"Unfortunately I don't speak a word of Arabic," I say, smiling sweetly at her.

"Amina means peace in Arabic."

"Yes, that's what I was guessing," I say, nodding. "Now shall we talk about your husband?"

I glance at Mason who's sitting about ten feet from us. He's already on his phone texting Raine.

Chapter Twenty

When Millie switched back to English, I knew she wanted me to hear something important. I'm already sending a text to Raine when she looks over.

Amina means peace in Arabic. Mir could be Amina.
Millie's not showing her cards yet, but it seems like that's
where she's headed.

Raine texts back to say she's starting to pull records on Amina. I tune back into Millie's conversation.

"So you have no idea where Amar is?" Millie settles back into her chair. Amina sits up straighter. The friendlier and more relaxed Millie gets, the more uncomfortable she gets. I'm guessing that's what Millie wants.

"I don't," Amina says, looking down. "He didn't give me any indication he was leaving, but it might have had something to do with a fight we had."

"What was the fight about?" Millie says. Her face looks almost uninterested. She's so good at this.

"You."

"Me?" Millie puts her hand over her chest. "I can't imagine why you and Amar would be talking about me, much less fighting about me."

"We've talked about you many times over the years. He was always much too concerned about you. He told me he was just worried about an old friend's daughter, but I always suspected there was more."

"What more could there be?" Millie frowns and tilts her head. She's playing innocent almost too well, but Amina seems to be buying it. "I met Amar for the first time when I questioned him in Sarajevo. What's it been now? Almost a year ago?"

"Yes, I remember when the men came to our house to get him," she says, gesturing over to Butch and me. I'm sure she doesn't remember our faces, but I guess we do all kind of look alike. "My youngest daughter was still living with us at that time. She was scared out of her mind, but Amar couldn't wait to go with them, so he would get to see you again. Somehow he knew you would be there. It's almost like you were in touch."

"I assure you, we were not. I didn't even know Amar knew my mother. At that point, I didn't even know for certain who my mother was." Millie shifts a bit in her seat. I can't tell if she's getting uncomfortable or if she's doing it for effect. I'm guessing the latter.

Amina looks at her coldly. I guess the small talk is over. "And have you been in touch with him since?"

"No, but I'm curious as to why you would think we would be in touch."

"Well," Amina says, pausing, "I guess when you find out who your real father is, you might want to talk to him."

Millie smiles. "Amina, Amar is not my father. I'm not sure what you think you know, but if you took one look at my real father, you'd know I belong to him."

"You look very much like your mother. Her hair was darker, but you have her green eyes. Yours are a little bit lighter, but they certainly have the same wide-eyed, innocent expression." Amina crosses her arms. "But genetics can be tricky. I find finances to be less so."

"Finances?"

"Yes, dear. My husband left you a quarter of our wealth in his will—his new will. I found it last week. In the original will, he left everything to me. In the new will, he's split it evenly between his four children—his three legitimate children with me and then his illegitimate child with Nejra."

Millie laughs and shakes her head. "Amina, I'm not Amar's child. I have no idea why he would leave me money. No offense, but I can't believe it's that much anyway. He's a dentist, not a baron of industry."

"Oh dear, please tell me you're not that lightly informed. I would expect better of a CIA agent. My family is very wealthy. That's why Amar married me after your uncle left. Amar's family was poor. I guess if he couldn't have your mother for love, he settled for me and the money. And in our world, all my money becomes the property of my husband. That never bothered me until I realized that my children would have to split their inheritance with you."

Millie sighs. "They won't have to share anything with me. I have no interest in your money. Even if he leaves me money —for whatever bizarre reason—I won't accept it. Your kids can split my portion—"

"Perhaps, we can get that in writing," Amina says, leaning forward.

"I'm more than happy to sign away any claims to your husband's inheritance," Millie says. "But do you really think that's why he disappeared? Because he didn't want to deal with your objections to the will?"

"We did get into a rather large fight about it," she says, eyeing Millie suspiciously. "What other reason could there be? The police tell me that a cab driver left him at the port. Do you have any more information as to where he went after that?"

"I don't. We just arrived right before we headed over here. Frankly, if his disappearance is for personal reasons, I have no reason to be here at all. The agency thought Amar might have had more to do with Sayid's network, but it doesn't look like that's the case."

"What do you mean by that?" Amina's eyes widen. From ten feet away, I can see she's getting nervous. I'm sure Millie's picking up on it.

"The agency has volumes and volumes of Sayid's old journals. He recorded everything. Apparently, he had a contact on the ground somewhere in Europe. They thought it might be Amar, but I've never believed that." Millie stands up suddenly. "If you don't have anything more to add, we'll leave you in peace. The agency will pass Amar's missing-person case back to the local police. Good luck. I hope you find him soon and that you can work out your differences."

Amina stands up, forgetting about the tea she has balanced in her lap. The cup and saucer fall to the floor, spraying tea all over her white dress. She looks up at Millie. All her cool confidence is gone. "How clumsy of me! I was surprised by how quickly you're leaving."

Millie bends over and collects a few of the larger chunks of the shattered china and puts them on the table. "Yes, I'm afraid our work is done. If Amar wasn't Sayid's contact, it could be anyone. Who knows? Back to the drawing board, I guess. Thank you for hosting us. It was so lovely talking to you."

Millie glides over to us as Amina struggles to follow her through the mess on the floor. "Perhaps we can meet again. I'm happy to have my attorney draw up papers for you to reject Amar's will."

Millie stops and turns around. "You know, you're right. Genetics can be tricky. Maybe I should get a blood test just to make sure. We'll be in Rome for a few days. I think you're in touch with my colleague Brad Simmons. Let him know when Amar gets back and we can get that out of the way."

Millie smiles as she floats through the elevator door that Butch is holding open for her. Amina's glaring at her. She takes a step toward Millie. I block her as I back into the elevator. She sputters as she looks from us to the tea stain on her dress. As the door closes, her eyes harden into a glare. She took the bait. She's definitely coming back after Millie at some point. Now, we just have to wait.

Chapter Twenty-One

"Are you certain?" Azayiz said as she wiped the tears off Nejra's face.

Nejra nodded as she looked into her aunt's concerned eyes. "Yes, Aza. It has to be. I haven't had my monthly in almost three months. I've missed it before, but never this long. And, I've been sick in the mornings—"

"You told me the American used condoms—"

"He did—every time. I don't know how it happened."

"It doesn't matter how it happened," Aza said, rubbing Nejra's back. "We're here and we have to decide what to do about it. Does anyone else know?"

"No." Nejra hesitated. "But I want to send a letter to Mack to tell him he has a baby on the way."

"Nejra," Aza said. "I don't think that's a good idea. As you said, I'm sure he had feelings for you, but he used condoms for a reason. He doesn't want a baby."

Nejra looked down and sighed. "He said he didn't want a baby—at least not yet."

"Child, you need to stop thinking about him. He was a ship that passed in the night. We need to come up with a realistic solution."

"There is no solution—"

"There is a solution for everything," Aza said, smiling. "You must get married. And we must act like you've been married for months."

"Married? I don't want to get married. Not to anyone here." Nejra started pacing. "And besides, who would marry me once they find out? I'm almost three months pregnant at this point."

"You know who would marry you—"

Nejra whipped around. "Yusef? Never! His family is so conservative. They would kill me if they found out I had relations before marriage. Even if they thought it was his baby."

"I'm not talking about Yusef. We have to keep this from him and his family. I'm talking about Amar."

"Amar? But, he's my best friend—"

"Child," Aza said, shaking her head. "You cannot be that blind. Amar has been in love with you since you were children. He would set himself on fire for you. But we must tell him that the American forced himself on you—"

"What? No! He did not force himself on me. In fact, it was just the opposite. He gave me every opportunity to turn away. I was the one who pursued him."

"Nejra, you have told me this and I believe you, but we are dealing with male egos. We must manage them. Amar—not to mention your brother—will be much more comfortable with helping you if they think you are a victim."

"That's ridiculous. You know they will think I'm ruined even if I was raped."

"Maybe, but they will adapt. You are the center of both of their worlds. They will protect you." Aza held Nejra's face in her hands. "Amar will marry you. He will be disappointed, but he will do this."

Nejra took a deep breath. "I don't want to marry Amar. I don't think of him like that—at all."

"It is our only solution to protect you and the baby." Aza stood up and walked toward the door. "And even then, you might be in danger. We need to hide you in this house until the baby is born. We will tell Sayid of our plan at dinner tonight. It's the only way. You know that."

Nejra nodded as Aza left the room, the tears coming back to her eyes.

***

"Was it at your job?" Sayid was furious. He had been pacing since Aza told him that Nejra was pregnant. "I told you that job would be no good! Do you know the man? I will kill him."

"He is an American and he is long gone now," Aza said, holding Nejra's hand firmly under the table. "Nejra doesn't know his name."

Sayid whipped around to face Nejra. "You didn't tell me there would be Americans at your job. And you said, you wouldn't have exposure to men—"

"Sayid!" Aza slammed her hand on the table. "It does us

no good to relive the past. It is done. We are here now. We have to come up with a plan to save your sister and the baby. If certain people find out, you know what they will expect you to do."

"No one will expect me to kill her," Sayid said, turning away from them. "We do not live in ancient times—"

"We don't," Aza said, "but others still do. You know that. Haroun Hadzic appointed himself your surrogate father after your parents died. How do you think he would handle this news?"

Sayid sat back down at the table. "He cannot know this. Or Yusef or any of their family. We have to find a way to hide it from them."

"Nejra and I have a plan," Aza said. "Amar will marry her. We will have to act like they were married months ago, but I know Amar will agree to it."

Sayid looked back at Nejra. "You have agreed to this?"

Nejra nodded, looking down. "It is the only way."

Sayid took an extended breath. "We will have to find a cleric who will lie for us. I'm not sure we can do that."

"Yes, that is an obstacle," Aza said. "Until then, we need to keep Nejra secluded. She will start showing soon."

Sayid nodded. "I will talk to Amar and tell him of our intentions. He will agree to it. He has been in love with Nejra since we were children. Even if this works, I think it would be best for us to leave Sarajevo. We need to live in a place where people will not question the story. One of my old school teachers lives just across the sea in a small fishing village in Italy. I will contact him and see if he would sponsor our immigration."

Aza nodded. "I think that is a good idea. Fareed and I are planning to move back to Pakistan to be with our family there. It is time we all left here."

Nejra looked up and smiled at them. She had to go along with their plans for now, but she had already decided to send a letter to Mack. Despite what Aza said, she knew he would come for her.

Chapter Twenty-Two

MILLIE, ROME, ITALY, 2020

As we crawl back in the van, Raine's waiting with her laptop turned toward us. She's pointing at the screen.

"Amina Petrovic is "Mir." I'm positive. She's traveled back and forth to Kabul for decades. I don't know how we missed it. Her travel paperwork says she was visiting family. I've identified a great uncle who lived there at one time. But from what I can tell, he was only there for a year on business. He lives in Sarajevo now. Our agents are tracking him down to question him. How did you leave it with her?"

"She's mad—which is good. It'll push her to make a move and hopefully make a mistake," I say as I take the laptop and start flipping through the travel records. "Apparently, Amar left me some money in his will—specifically some of her family's money. I let her believe I was considering taking it. I told her I was going to get a blood test to prove paternity. She's convinced I'm Amar's daughter."

Raine touches my arm. "Millie, that doesn't mean—"

"It doesn't mean anything. I'm not his daughter. I don't know what he's playing at, but I'm not his daughter." I look around. Everyone's looking down. "I'm not his daughter—end of discussion. Can we get our focus back on the mission? I dropped some information about Sayid's journals. She knows he wrote about his ground contact. She doesn't know if he named her. She's scared. She'll make a move."

"Brad's already set a watch around her house," Raine says.

"Yeah, we need to wait to see what she does. If she doesn't take the bait, I'll come back over here and whip her up a little bit more."

Raine nods as we all settle in for the ride to our villa. Mason's squeezing my hand extra tight. I know he's starting to believe Amar might be my dad. If we were alone, I would get into it with him, but now's not the time. And frankly, I'm too tired to even concentrate on it right now. The van pulls up to a gated villa on a quiet, tree-lined street. I'm assuming this is one of the agency's safe houses.

"Not much protection here," Hawk says, looking up and down the street as Brad opens the courtyard gate for us.

"It's Rome, not the Middle East," Brad says. "We like to try to blend in here. As far as anyone's concerned, you're tourists. Raine, our command center is set up in the guest house over there. Sorry, Millie, you don't have agency credentials anymore. You won't have access."

"Brad—"

"No, Raine, it's fine," I say, looking from Brad to her. "He's right. Have at it and let me know if you need anything."

"The entire third floor is yours—four bedrooms and a

sitting area," Brad says, nodding at the front door. "There's an elevator to the left as you walk in."

The guys and I head upstairs and throw our bags in rooms. Mason follows me into a bedroom and puts his bag next to mine. I guess we're sharing a room. He looks over and sees me looking down at his bag.

"We can share a room. It's no big deal." He closes the door behind us. "Are you going to take a nap?"

"Yeah."

"Do you want me to stay up here with you?" He pulls me into a hug.

"Mase, we can't have sex," I say against his chest. "We need to keep some level of professionalism."

He pushes me back, laughing. "I think only one of us is talking about sex right now."

I roll my eyes. "I'm pretty sure both of us are thinking about it."

"Yeah, guilty." He grabs my shoulders and gets down on my eye level. "Now, do you want to talk about why Amar Petrovic named you in his will?"

"No," I say, spinning away from him. "Don't tell me you think he's my dad. I thought we were on the same page."

"We are on the same page, but I think it's weird that you're in his will. I mean, what other reason could he have for doing that?"

"I don't know," I say, falling onto the bed. "Maybe he feels guilty about something related to Mom."

"We haven't seen the will." He sits down next to me and starts rubbing my stomach. Somehow, he always anticipates when it's getting upset. "Maybe his wife was lying about it."

"No, she wasn't lying. It's the reason she wanted to talk to me. She doesn't want any of her family money going to me. My name's definitely in the will. We just have to figure out why."

"I guess the only person who knows why is Amar. God knows where he is by now," he says. "Mills, maybe when we get back, you should have a blood test and find out for sure."

"What?" I say, moving his hand off my stomach. "Are you being serious right now?"

"No, I mean, just to verify it, so you don't have to worry about it—"

"I'm not worried about it," I say, standing up. "You shouldn't be either. I know who my dad is."

"Mills," he says, reaching for my hand. I pull away from him. "C'mon. You know that's the way I'm built. I like to know things for certain. Don't be mad at me."

I shake my head. "I'm not mad at you. I don't want to do that to Dad. He told me a long time ago he had a paternity test done. I don't want to question him—"

"He's lied to you before—"

"Mason!" I spin around and glare at him. "Seriously, stop. I'm taking a nap. I don't want to talk about this anymore."

He follows me into the sitting room. The sun's coming through the open terrace doors and landing in a warm puddle on the couch. I collapse down onto it and pull a few pillows under my head.

"Baby," he says, stroking my hair.

"Mase, please. Let's talk about it later. I'm so tired." My eyes start to tear up. I've been so emotional since Dad got back. I'm hoping that's going to go away soon.

"You've been tired a lot lately. Maybe you should go to the doctor when we get back."

"I'm fine. This last month has just been more than my mind can take. Can I please take a nap?"

"Okay, baby." He pulls a blanket over me and tucks it under my chin. "I'm going down to the courtyard to have a beer with the guys. Will you join us when you wake up?"

"Yeah," I say as I close my eyes. A tear escapes from my eye and rolls down my cheek. Mason stops it with a kiss. When he starts to stand up, I grab his arm.

"I love you, Mase," I say as I smile up at him.

"I love you, baby." He leans over and kisses my forehead. "More than anything in the world."

As I roll over and close my eyes again, I hear him closing the door softly as he heads downstairs. I'm about to drift off to sleep when I hear the door opening again.

"Mase, I'm fine."

I roll over to see Amar Petrovic standing across the room with a gun in his hand.

"Amar," I say slowly.

He takes a few steps toward me. His eyes are red and swollen. "We could have been so happy. I would have been such a good father to you."

"Amar." I push myself up as he raises the gun. "Put the gun down. Let's talk about this."

"I'm so tired of talking." He turns around and starts walking to the other side of the room. I'm about ready to run for the door when he turns back around and raises the gun to his temple. "I'm so tired of everything."

"Amar, no!" I jump up and put my arms out as I slowly

walk toward him. "Don't. Please don't do this. My mom wouldn't want you to do this."

"Yes, she would—after what I did to her—"

"Amar." As I take another step toward him, he looks down —his arm dropping slightly. I spring forward and tackle him to the ground. The gun fires as I land on top of him.

Chapter Twenty-Three

MASON, ROME, ITALY 2020

As I head down to the courtyard, I can't get the image of Millie out of my mind—lying on the couch, her teary green eyes shining up at me. All I want to do is curl up with her and protect her from reality—from everything. I almost turn around, but I promised the guys I'd have a beer with them, so I continue down the stairs.

"Where's Mills?" Butch asks as I walk outside. He and Hawk are stretched out on lounge chairs, drinking Peronis.

"She's sprawled out just like you, but on the couch upstairs. She's been really tired lately."

"It's not from the amount of work we've done here," Hawk says. "This has been the easiest mission of my career. I could get used to it."

"You only have six months until you retire," I say. "This is probably what the rest of your life's going to look like. Do you know what your plans are yet?"

"No idea, man." Hawk sighs. "My daughter's living out in

Vegas now. I don't have a reason to stay in Virginia. Who knows? Maybe I'll join you out in California. How about you, Butch? Are you going back to Georgia?"

"Naw," he says as he takes a long draw on this beer. "Georgia's done for me. After what we've seen and done for the past couple decades, it's hard to go home."

"Well you're both welcome out in San Diego. We've got a nice little community going out there."

"Maybe Millie can get us some more of these cushy assignments as freelancers," Butch laughs. "I feel like the only thing missing is a woman feeding me grapes—"

That's when we hear the gunshot—just one—coming from upstairs where Millie's sleeping on the couch. Within seconds, we have our pistols drawn and are charging up the stairs. When I bust through the door, I see Millie on the floor on top of a man. She's wrestling with him—trying to get a gun out of his hand. I don't have a clear shot.

Millie jerks her head around when she hears us come in. Instead of rolling off him, she spreads her body fully out on top of him.

"Don't shoot him!" she screams. "Don't shoot him. He's not going to hurt me."

Butch and Hawk have already fanned out to the sides of the room. "Hawk, you got a shot?" I ask as I keep my gun raised. I still don't have a clear shot around Millie.

"Yep, just tell me when," Hawk says.

"Amar," Millie says. "Let go of the gun. These guys will kill you. Please. Think about your kids. Think about me."

Amar looks up at her—his eyes dazed. He takes a deep, shaky breath and slowly loosens his grip on the gun. Butch jumps toward them and snatches the gun out of Amar's hand. I grab Millie around the waist and pull her away as Hawk lands on top of Amar.

I press Millie a little too roughly against the wall. "What the fuck were you thinking? You know we come into these rooms hot. Don't you ever put yourself between me and an armed man again! Do you understand me? I could have shot you, Millie."

Her eyes tear up when she hears the booming, angry tone in my voice. I take a deep breath and pull her into a hug. "Mills, it's okay. I'm sorry I yelled at you," I say more softly. She's crying harder now—making little sobbing noises. It's tearing me apart. "Baby, I was just scared. I'm sorry. Okay? God, I could have shot you. Never do that again. Please. Promise me."

She nods her head against my chest. I know I should probably make her vocalize the promise, but she's crying so hard. The guilt's exploding through my body. I've never made her cry. Not once. In fact, since I've known her, I've only seen her cry a couple of times. But since we got back from Pakistan, she tears up at everything. I thought it was because her dad was back, but I'm beginning to think there's more to it.

"Mase, we need to call the local police," Butch says.

"No, not yet." Millie pulls back from me—tears still falling down her cheeks. "I need to talk to Amar—"

"Not happening," I say as gently as I can. I block her from Amar who's now sitting on the couch with his hands cuffed behind him. Hawk's towering over him.

"Mase, I need to talk to him. You know why." She's looking up at me. Her eyes are so upset. "You can stay in the room—guns drawn, if necessary. Just give me a little space. I have to know."

I nod. "Hawk, position yourself across the room. If he so much as looks at her wrong, take him out. Butch, find Raine. She went to the guest house when we got back."

I escort Millie over to the couch. She sits down facing him. I sit in the chair right next to them. Millie looks up at me.

"You can have exactly five feet of space. That's it." I'm waiting for her to challenge me. She doesn't.

She looks back at Amar. "Amar," she says softly. "Why were you trying to kill yourself?"

"I deserve to die after what I did to your mom—to you." He looks down.

"What did you do?"

He shakes his head and looks back up at her—a slight smile coming to his face. "Did you know we were married— your mom and me?"

"I didn't know that." Millie's voice is shaky. I want to reach out to her, but I don't. She's working. She'd be pissed if I interrupted her. "When did you get married?"

"Two days before you were born." He's smiling broadly now. I can't see Millie's face, but I'm sure she's not sharing his glee. "Did you know you were born early? She wasn't due for another month. Or at least that's what we thought. Nejra was having problems. We thought we were going to lose her— and you—that night."

"Why did you marry her, Amar? I'm not your daughter." Her voice is still shaky.

He ignores her question. "Nejra was in so much pain. Sayid was beside himself. That's why he had me get Mrs.

Hadzic. If she hadn't come over to help us that night, no one would have known about you. We hid Nejra's pregnancy for all those months. We would have been off to Italy before anyone knew. We had it all planned out. It would have worked if you hadn't come early. We thought she was going to die. We had to get help. We would have been so happy—such a happy family."

"Amar." She reaches out and touches his knee. Everything about that pisses me off. Even though he's cuffed, I still don't want her that close to him, but I know it's an interrogation technique. "I'm not your daughter. Why did you marry her?"

He ignores her again. "I saw you at our house earlier. I never left Rome. I've been watching the house, waiting for her to make a move."

"Who? Amina? What do you mean 'make a move'?"

"She never got over him—your uncle. After all these years, she's still deeply in love with him. That's why she did it. She would have done anything for him. I knew that, but I never thought she'd go this far. But I would have done anything for Nejra, too, so I guess I understand." He's rambling. His eyes are all over the place.

Millie scoots back a little on the couch. "What did she do? And how do you know?"

He focuses back on Millie. "I found her records. I was going through her jewelry box looking for the first engagement ring I gave her. It belonged to my mom and then I gave it to Nejra. I wanted you to have it." He pauses for a second. "The flash drive was right there in her jewelry box."

"What's on the flash drive?" Millie glances over to see if Raine's in the room. She just arrived with Butch and Brad.

"It has records on it—records of what she did for Sayid," Amar says, looking up at the ceiling and sighing. "She worked for him for decades. I had no idea. How could I have been so stupid?"

"Where's the flash drive, Amar?"

He looks back at her and then looks around the room. His eyes are getting panicky again. "It's safe. She noticed it was missing and searched my office. That's when she found my new will. Did she tell you about the will? I put you in it."

"Amar," Millie says in a harsh tone that I've never heard from her. "Where's the flash drive?"

Butch walks over to search him again. Hawk patted him down for weapons and explosives, but he didn't do a deep search. Millie waves Butch back.

"If I give you the drive, you will end our conversation," Amar says slowly. "I have more I need to tell you."

"We can talk more, but you need to tell me where the drive is first." She smiles at him. "You can trust me."

Amar nods. "It's in the left internal pocket of my jacket."

After Butch gives the drive to Brad, I walk over to Amar. His nose has started to bleed from where Hawk punched him. I grab the tissues from the table and push one up the nostril that's bleeding. As subtly as I can, I tear a small blood-stained piece off.

"Watch him," I say to Hawk as I follow Raine, Butch, and Brad out the door. "Raine, wait."

She's halfway down the stairs. I walk down to her and hand her the tiny piece of tissue. "Test it against Millie."

"Mason." Her eyes widen as she shakes her head.

"Do I have to ask you again?" My voice lowers into a low growl as I shove the tissue into her hand.

"No." She takes it and heads back down the stairs where Butch is waiting to escort them back to the guest house.

"The results only come to me," I say to her back.

She stops and looks over her shoulder. "I understand," she says as she turns back around.

Chapter Twenty-Four

SARAJEVO, BOSNIA, 1995

"Where is Aza?" Nejra groaned as tears streamed down her face. She had been in labor most of the day but had tried to ignore it. The baby wasn't due for another month. Within the last hour, the pain had gotten so much worse. With every contraction, she seemed to lose a little more touch with reality.

"Nejra, you know she went back to Pakistan for her father's funeral." Sayid was trying to calm her down, but panic was starting to rise in his voice. "She left a week ago. Do you remember?"

Nejra screamed as the next contraction hit. "The baby is coming too early. Make it stop."

"Go get Mrs. Hadzic," Sayid said to Amar. "She's done this before. We need her."

"Sayid, are you sure?" Amar said, cringing as Nejra screamed again. "She will tell her husband. You know how he will react—what he will expect of you."

"We don't have a choice," Sayid said as he wiped the

sweat off Nejra's forehead. "She will die here if we don't do something."

Amar took one more look at Nejra's anguished face and then rushed out the door.

"Mrs. Hadzic will help us," Sayid whispered to Nejra. "It will all be fine. Keep your mind on Italy. We will be there with the baby soon."

After Nejra waited months for Mack to respond to her letter, she reluctantly agreed to marry Amar two days ago. She knew it was the only way to survive. After the baby was born, they were moving to Italy. Although she wasn't happy about marrying Amar, Nejra was excited for a fresh start in another country.

Sayid turned toward the door as Mrs. Hadzic rushed in. She glared at Sayid but softened her face as she approached Nejra.

"Nejra," she whispered. "I am here now. Everything is going to work out. The baby is just eager to see you."

Nejra smiled slightly through her tears as she nodded at Mrs. Hadzic.

"Get me hot water, clean towels, and a sterilized knife," Mrs. Hadzic said to Sayid and Amar. "Now!"

Sayid and Amar ran out of the bedroom door to the kitchen. When they returned with the supplies, Nejra had her legs propped up on the bed with Mrs. Hadzic looking between them. They both stopped in their tracks.

Mrs. Hadzic glared at them. "It is a baby being born—a natural process. Get yourselves together and help me. Sayid, support Nejra's back."

"She is my wife," Amar said quickly. "I will do that."

Mrs. Hadzic turned her head to him. "Your wife? And when did this happen?"

"Almost a year ago—in a private ceremony." Amar sat down on the bed and wrapped his arms around Nejra's shoulders.

Mrs. Hadzic nodded, but she could tell from the awkward way he touched her that he was lying. She knew she would have to tell her husband about all of this. And she also knew what that would likely mean, but she didn't have time to consider it now. Nejra's mother had been her best friend. She had to try to keep her daughter alive.

"The baby's head is showing, Nejra," Mrs. Hadzic said. "I need you to push as hard as you can."

"I'm so tired," Nejra whined as she tried to breathe through the pain.

"Nejra," Sayid said as he took her hand again. "Forget everything and everybody except me. We will do this together. Squeeze my hand as hard as you can and push with everything you have inside of you."

Nejra nodded as she locked her eyes with his and pushed. After several tries, she heard a cry. She opened her eyes and looked down. Mrs. Hadzic was wrapping her baby in towels.

"Is he alive?" Nejra whimpered.

"It is a girl. She is alive and healthy." Mrs. Hadzic smiled. "Maybe a little bit small, but big enough to survive on her own."

The baby wailed as Mrs. Hadzic wiped her face gently. "She seems to have a lot to say already," Mrs. Hadzic said. "She takes after your mother."

"Yes, I think she does," Nejra said as Mrs. Hadzic laid the

baby on her chest. "I'm going to name her after Momma. She looks like a Yasmine."

Mrs. Hadzic looked at Sayid and Amar. "Please take all of these dirty towels and destroy them. Don't throw them out. Destroy them. I'm going to stay the night with Nejra to make sure the baby stays healthy. You may sleep somewhere else."

After she shooed them out the door, she looked at Nejra. She turned her eyes to the ceiling and silently begged Nejra's mother for forgiveness. She knew what was likely coming, and that she was powerless to stop it. She hoped Sayid had a plan to take Nejra away from here, but she knew she couldn't participate.

"Nejra," she said, walking over to the bed. "She's crying because she's hungry."

"Already?" Nejra said, looking up at her with wide eyes.

"Yes, she seems to have a big appetite. Let me show you how to feed her."

After a few tries, Yasmine latched on successfully. Nejra laughed at the very active way she was eating. As she leaned down to kiss the top of Yasmine's head, she noticed a few red hairs. She covered the baby quickly with the blanket so Mrs. Hadzic couldn't see, but she already knew it was too late. Yasmine had the fairest skin she had ever seen—it was almost translucent. She and Amar had olive skin. There was no way they could have made this baby.

Chapter Twenty-Five

Mason walks back in as Hawk's taking the cuffs off Amar.

"What the fuck?" Mason says, running across the room.

Hawk stops him. "His nose is bleeding harder. He needs his hands unless we want the blood all over the couch. I won't let him get near her."

"Millie, switch seats," Mason says. "Take the chair I was sitting in. I want you further away from him. And let's wrap this up quickly."

I nod at him as I sit in his chair. He's standing right behind me.

"Amar, we don't have a lot of time," I say, looking back at him. "You need to get to a hospital, and then the authorities are going to want to question you. You keep saying you did something to my mom. What did you do?"

He takes a long breath and holds it for a second. His face starts to get flush before he finally releases it slowly. "I married your mother two days before she gave birth. She finally realized your father wasn't coming for her, so she agreed to marry me. Sayid was our only witness. It was a legal wedding—officiated by a cleric. He went to school with us. He was a friend. He ignored that Nejra was obviously pregnant. We were going to move to Italy after you were born. Sayid was coming with us. We had it all planned out."

His voice trails off as his eyes glaze over.

"But I'm not your daughter. I know I'm not, Amar. I'm guessing you never even had sex with her."

He lowers his eyes, but doesn't say anything.

"You said she realized my dad wasn't coming for her, but she never tried to contact him—"

"She did," Amar says, dabbing more blood off his cheek. "She wrote him a letter."

My heart stops for a second. I think I know where this is going. "He never got a letter," I say.

"I know." He looks up at me—his eyes pleading for understanding. "She gave it to me to mail."

I put my hands over my face. "Tell me you mailed it, Amar," I whisper, but I already know he didn't.

"I burned it." He barely gets it out before I leap out of my chair and backhand him hard across the face.

My hand barely makes contact with him when Mason wraps his arms around my waist and lifts my flailing body off the ground—pulling me to the other side of the room.

"You motherfucker!" I scream, pointing at Amar as Mason drags me farther back. "You let her die thinking my dad didn't care about her."

"Whoa, Mills," Mason whispers. "Whoa."

Amar starts to stand up. Hawk shoves him back down roughly.

"No! I told her what I did! Right after you were born," Amar says, holding his hand over the bright red mark that's developing on his cheek. "We were already married. She was so mad at me. She said she was going to send him another letter and divorce me when he came for her. I yelled at her. He never could have loved her the way I did. But in the end, she knew the truth. I knew you needed to know the truth, too."

"You confessed to make yourself feel better. Do you think knowing this makes me feel any better?" I try to pry Mason's arms from around me. "My dad would have come for her. He would have brought her back to the U.S. We could have been a family, you fucking coward."

He's starting to cry again. "We fought after I told her the truth. When I left, you were sleeping on her chest. I came back to apologize and—"

"And what?" I say, slumping into Mason's arms. He wraps them tighter around me so I won't fall to the ground. "And what, Amar? Did you kill her?"

Amar jerks his head up to look at me. "No! I loved her. She's the only woman I've ever loved, still to this day, but—"

"But what?" I'm so tired—my mind, my body. It's all too much. My head's spinning. I feel like I'm going to faint.

Amar looks down at his lap. "I was there—when it happened—when he killed her." He's whispering. I can barely hear him. "I could have stopped it if I reacted more quickly. If—"

I take a long, shaky breath. "If what, Amar? Who killed her?"

"Haroun Hadzic. He smothered her. I saw him." He shakes his head violently, probably trying to get rid of the memory of Haroun killing Mom while he did nothing. "She didn't suffer. She didn't even wake up. It's like it happened in slow motion. He put a pillow over her face. She didn't fight back. She didn't move. I think Haroun's wife might have put some kind of sleeping medication in her tea. He held the pillow there for a few minutes and then just walked away. I could have stopped him, but I froze. And you were on her chest. I thought he had already killed you. After he left, I went in. She was dead, but you were still alive—sleeping so peacefully."

I start shaking—my body's vibrating against Mason's chest.

"Millie, come on," Mason whispers to me as he starts pulling me toward the door. "Let's get out of here."

I plant my feet to try to stop him. "No, Mason. Not yet."

He stops but doesn't let go of me. "You don't need to hear anymore."

"I do. Let go of me. I'm fine." He loosens his arms but stays glued to me as I walk toward Amar. I take out my cell phone and start the recorder. "Tell me the entire story of how she died, Amar."

Chapter Twenty-Six

SARAJEVO, BOSNIA, 1995

Nejra finished feeding Yasmine and laid her down on her chest for a nap. Yasmine was not even a week old, but she already had an enormous appetite. Nejra fed her at least once an hour. It was exhausting, but Nejra loved the alone time with her baby. Sayid and Amar would, of course, leave the room during feeding time. Nejra pretended it took longer than it did, so she could be alone with Yasmine.

Since Nejra married Amar, she didn't want to look at him. The thought of spending the rest of her life with him was almost crushing. She didn't love him—not like that. He had been her best friend since she was a little girl, but she didn't desire him at all. She hadn't wanted to marry him, but she knew it was the only way. Mack hadn't responded to her letter. She didn't understand why. Even in the short time they spent together, she thought she knew him deeply. She was disappointed, but she knew she had to move on. Despite her best efforts, she still thought about Mack, especially when she looked at Yasmine's red hair.

"Nejra," Amar said, knocking lightly on the door. "Are you done? Mrs. Hadzic is here to see you."

"Yes, the baby is sleeping," she said softly.

Amar opened the door and peeked in. He smiled broadly as he walked in with Mrs. Hadzic following him.

"Nejra," Mrs. Hadzic said, passing by Amar. "I've made you some lemongrass tea. I know it was your favorite when your mother was alive. She always made it best, but I hope I've gotten close. Please drink the entire pot. It will help you heal more quickly."

Mrs. Hadzic had been at her side since she helped Nejra deliver the baby. She visited several times a day. Knowing how conservative her family was, it surprised Nejra that she wanted anything to do with her and Yasmine. Nejra wondered if she told her husband or son about the baby. They had hid it from their family the entire pregnancy. If she hadn't had a problem delivering the baby, even Mrs. Hadzic wouldn't have known until they were already in Italy. Although she was married now, she knew they wouldn't buy that Amar was the father, especially after looking at Yasmine.

"Thank you," Nejra said, sitting up as Mrs. Hadzic handed her a cup. She tried to take the baby from her, but Nejra resisted. "I can hold her and drink at the same time. I'm getting very good at it."

"A baby shouldn't be this reliant on its mother," Mrs. Hadzic said. "She will have to learn to fend for herself."

"She's not even a week old. She can be attached to me for at least a month," Nejra said, smiling.

Mrs. Hadzic looked away quickly. Nejra thought she looked sad and worried, but she couldn't understand why.

"Mrs. Hadzic, are you feeling well?" Nejra said as she drained her cup of tea.

Mrs. Hadzic tried her best to smile at Nejra. "Yes, dear. Have one more cup of tea and then I'll leave you to rest."

Nejra nodded, but she was already feeling sleepy. She wanted everyone to leave so she could rest with Yasmine. Mrs. Hadzic poured her another cup of tea. She touched Nejra's face gently. "Bless you, child. Your mother looks down on you and waits anxiously to see you again."

Nejra smiled as she watched her walk out of the room. She had been thinking about her mother all morning. She yearned to see her again—to introduce her to Yasmine.

Amar sat down on the couch next to her and stroked her arm. "Sayid said we should have enough money to get to Italy in another month. He's already contacted his old teacher who lives there now. He and his wife have offered us a room until we can get settled there."

Nejra nodded as she considered again whether to tell him of her intentions. "Amar," she said, "I must tell you something. I've decided to write to Yasmine's father again. I know he leads a busy life. I think he might have missed the letter I sent him. I want to give him another chance. I know he would want to see her—"

"Nejra." Amar's voice raised a few octaves. "We've already discussed that he wanted nothing more than to be with you—in that way. He has no interest in this child."

"I don't believe that, even for a second. I know him. You

146

don't. He is a decent man. I don't think he ever received the letter."

Amar stood up and started pacing in the small room. "We are married now. What will you do if he does want to be with the child? You can't go to America and he can't stay here. It's better that he doesn't know."

"What do you mean 'that he doesn't know'? You and Sayid told me that he does know and that he just doesn't care."

"I mean that there is no reason to send him another letter. If he hasn't already ignored your first letter, he will likely ignore the second."

Nejra got a sinking feeling in her stomach. "Amar, did you mail the letter I gave you?"

"He has no right to be a part of this child's life. He took advantage of you and then abandoned you—"

"Amar! Please tell me you mailed the letter."

Amar stopped pacing and sat down next to Nejra again. Tears started coming to his eyes as he saw the shock and betrayal on her face. "We will be so happy in Italy, Nejra."

Nejra closed her eyes. She pulled Yasmine closer to her. "Get out, Amar. Get out of my house. I am done with you."

"Nejra, you are my wife—"

"Get out," Nejra whispered. "Get out. I never want to see you again. When I am well enough, I will divorce you no matter what it takes. I will write to him again. He will come to get me and our baby."

Amar looked at her one more time, but her eyes were closed. He decided to let her sleep and appeal to her senses later. He was halfway home when he turned around. He had betrayed her trust. He knew he owed her an apology. No matter what had happened, Nejra was his best friend. He would never let that change.

As he approached the house, he glanced in the front room window. He saw a man standing over Nejra's sleeping body. At first, he thought it was Sayid. He couldn't get a clear view through the dirty panes. The man grabbed a pillow off the floor and put it over her face. Nejra didn't struggle. When the man finally removed the pillow, he turned and saw Amar frozen at the window. Amar took a quick step back and tripped over a flower pot. As he tried to recover, the man walked out of the house.

"It is done," Haroun Hadzic said, looking down at Amar. "You will be next if you ever speak of it."

As Amar watched Haroun walk next door to his own house, he untangled himself from the flower pot and hesitantly walked into the house.

As he stepped into the room, he saw Nejra lying on the couch. Her beautiful, green eyes were open, but he already knew she was dead. He felt for a pulse. There wasn't one. With tears streaming down his face, he leaned down to kiss her and gently closed her eyes.

He took a quick breath when the baby stirred. He assumed that she was dead, too. He picked her up. Yasmine looked up at him—smiling—blissfully unaware of how her life had changed in the last few minutes.

"You are my daughter," he whispered to Yasmine. "I will raise you like one of my own. For the rest of my life, I will do everything I can to protect you."

Chapter Twenty-Seven

MASON, ROME, ITALY, 2020

Amar finished his story a few minutes ago, but Millie still hasn't said anything. She's just staring at him. The blank look on her face is breaking my heart into a million pieces.

"Millie, let's get out of here," I say, trying to turn her toward the door again. She's leaning with her back against my chest. Her body's limp. I'm not even sure she can move right now. "Baby, come on."

"You have to forgive me, Millie," Amar says so quietly I can barely hear him. If he didn't look so pathetic right now, I would tear him apart.

"Mason," Millie says. She takes a deep breath as her body comes to life again. "Let me go. I'm fine."

As I loosen my grip on her, she walks back over to Amar and stands over him. I follow her and stand inches from her. I'm not sure if she's going to hit him again or faint, but I'm pretty sure something's going to happen.

"No, I don't have to forgive you, Amar, but I will because I don't want this hanging over me for one second longer. I want you gone. I want you to leave me and my dad alone. You're not a part of my life. You never were. Take me out of your will. Get me out of your mind. If you ever contact me again, I swear to God, I'll kill you."

I put my hand on her shoulder. She knocks it off as she turns toward the door. Amar's still crying.

"Millie, please," he begs. "She would have been happy with me. I had to make a choice."

Millie spins back around and starts charging at him again. I step in front of her.

"It was her choice, not yours," she says, pointing at Amar as she tries to get around me. "You took that choice away from her."

"I know that now," he whispers. "It haunts me."

She shakes her head and takes another deep breath. "Bottom line, it's been twenty-five years. It's over. All of this is over. Move on with your life. I have. My dad has. If you want to do anything to make it up to me, get beyond it. We're done. Just because you were a part of Mom's life, doesn't mean you're part of mine. You got me to my dad when I was a baby. I know she's happy about that. It's over now. Accept that and I will be content."

He nods his head. "I will accept that. I will leave you alone now."

Millie walks out of the room without saying anything more to him. I follow her down the stairs and to the guest house where the agency has set up shop.

"I guess that's that," Brad says as we walk into the room.

"Good work, Millie. Hopefully, that's it for this network. We're still going through the files, but we have enough to arrest Amina. The police are on their way to pick her up now. The Italian government won't let us take her until they've interviewed her, but we've got her. Excellent work. The director's happy."

Millie smiles at him and nods her head. I can tell she's trying not to break down. After Amar told her he burned the letter her mom tried to send to Mack, Millie's entire posture changed. She did a good job hiding her distress from Amar, but I can tell she's just holding on right now.

Hawk walks in. "The cops just took Amar."

"You know, the five of us make a good team," Butch says, leaning against the wall and smiling. "Maybe we could do our own version of Hawaii Five-O when Hawk and I retire."

"Five-O stands for Hawaii being the fiftieth state in the union, not the number of people," Raine says, laughing.

"I'm going for a walk," Millie says. "I need some fresh air."

Her voice is shrill and stressed. When I put my hand on her back, she recoils like a snake just bit her.

"You okay, Mills?" Butch looks at her, frowning.

"I'm fine," she says, getting her voice back almost to normal. "I just need to walk. Mason, you stay with them. I'll be back in a bit."

Everyone starts laughing and shaking their heads. "There's a better chance of the world exploding right now than Mason letting you take a walk by yourself," Hawk says. "Mase, you good? Or you need backup?"

"I've got her," I say, watching Millie out of the corner of

my eye as she walks toward the door. "Stay here and make sure these two are safe. We'll catch up with you later."

I turn on my heel and follow Millie. She's leaning against the front fence with her hands covering her face. I try to move her hands away.

"Don't," she says, shaking her head.

"Mills." I try to pull her hands down again.

She keeps her hands pressed to her eyes. Her body starts to shake again. "I just need some alone time," she says, her voice quivering.

"Millie, I'm sorry, but there's no way I'm letting you go anywhere alone right now," I say. "If you need to walk, go ahead. I'll follow you. You don't have to talk to me. You don't even have to walk by me, but I'm coming with you."

She stands up and takes her hands away from her red, teary eyes. "Okay, but I don't want to talk."

"Okay," I say as I open the gate for her.

She takes out down the street ahead of me. I try to give her a little space, but it's not easy. I can hear her crying. Her little sobs and sniffles are killing me. I want to hold her so badly right now. I'm following about five feet behind her when she stops and turns around. She walks back to me, tears streaming down her face. She drops her head onto my chest. I wrap my arms around her and hug her more tightly than I ever have before. She doesn't say anything or make any attempt to hug me back. We stand that way for a few minutes before she pulls back. She reaches for my hand. I lace my fingers firmly into hers.

"I still don't want to talk." She starts walking again, pulling me along with her.

"Okay, baby," I say as I squeeze her hand.

She wraps her other hand around my arm and lays her head against my shoulder as we keep walking up the street.

Chapter Twenty-Eight

MILLIE, ROME, ITALY, 2020

We've been walking for about ten minutes. He's squeezing my hand tightly, but he hasn't said anything. He knows my mind's in knots. He's giving me a few minutes to untangle it.

When we walk into a peaceful, little piazza, he guides me over to a bench next to a fountain. We sit down and watch a mother and her toddler daughter deciding what flavor to get from the gelato stand. He puts his arm around me and pulls me to him. He knows I'm thinking about Mom and what could have been as I watch them.

"Do you want to talk about it now?" he whispers.

I take a deep, shaky breath. "She died without knowing if Dad would have come for her."

"She knew. Believe me, she knew."

I look up at him. "Do you think?"

"Yeah," he says, wiping a tear off my cheek. "She knew Mack. She knew what kind of person he was. He would have taken out an entire army to get to her—to get to you. She knew that, and in the end, she knew he never got that chance."

"That's so sad though. She died knowing that."

"No, Mills, she didn't," he says, shaking his head. "From what Amar told us, she fell asleep thinking she was going to wake up in the morning and write Mack another letter. She died with hope and most importantly, she died with the love of her life sleeping on her chest. That's a beautiful way to go."

His crystal-blue eyes shine at me as a smile lights up his face. God, I love that face, that smile, those eyes.

"How did I get so lucky?" I say, smiling back at him.

"Lucky?" His forehead wrinkles up. "You lost your mom when you were a week old, not to mention all the crap you've been through these past nine years."

"Yeah, but despite all that, somehow I found you."

"Baby," he whispers as he pulls me in for a long, slow kiss. "I'm the lucky one. There's nothing I did right in my entire life that makes me deserve you, but I'll keep working at it. Anything you want, I'm going to get it for you. Anything."

"I want a gelato." I'm eyeing the little girl who now has gelato dripping down the front of her dress.

Mason laughs. "I was thinking more big picture than that, but yeah, I can get you a gelato. I know strawberry's your first choice. What do you want if they don't have it?"

"Surprise me." As I watch him walk away, I know I'm ready. Just like that, I know.

He turns around and smiles at me. "They don't have strawberry. Do you want pistachio or peach?"

"Yes."

"Mills," he says, laughing as he takes a few steps back toward me, "it's not a yes or no question."

"That's not the question I'm answering."

He walks the rest of the way over to me. "What? What question are you answering?"

"The one you asked me a couple of months ago," I say, "when we were sitting out on our back porch, eating burritos. Do you remember what you asked?"

He drops down on the bench and takes my hand. "Vividly and I remember what you answered."

I shrug and tilt my head. "Maybe you should ask again. The answer might be different this time."

"Millie," he says, pulling me onto his lap, "you know I want to marry you more than anything, but you've had one of the hardest days of your life. Maybe today isn't the day to make big decisions."

I smile at him. "What? Have you rescinded the question?"

"You know I haven't."

He's looking at me sternly. It's the look he uses when he's trying to discipline me. He should know by now that all it does is turn me on. I lean forward for a kiss. He kisses me for a few seconds and then pushes me back a little. He's squinting his eyes hard.

"Seriously?" I say, laughing. "You've been able to read my mind since the second I met you. You really don't know what I'm thinking right now?"

"I think I do," he says, searching my eyes for further clues. "Are you sure?"

"I guess you're not going to know unless you ask." As I stand up to walk toward the gelato stand, he grabs my hand

and spins me back around. He takes a deep breath and starts to lower onto his knee—

"Mason!" Both of our heads spin around to see Hawk running toward us. He looks like he's about to start a firefight right in the middle of this tiny piazza. He stops in front of us and takes a quick breath.

"What?" All the gentleness in Mason's face is gone instantly.

"JJ's dead."

My hand flies over my mouth as I try to process the news.

"How?" Mason says. His face is already battle-ready.

Hawk shakes his head. "On a mission. Bryce said he was all over the place—went into a room too early—"

"Did they take the other guys out?" Mason growls as his fists clench tightly.

"They got a few. They're in pursuit of the others right now. They want us there. We're wheels up in an hour. I've been trying to call you. You didn't answer. I tracked you here."

Mason nods his head slowly. "Give me a second," he says, looking at Hawk.

"You've got five minutes. It'll take them that long to get the car here." Hawk takes a few steps back and gets on his phone.

Mason closes his eyes and takes a deep breath.

"Mason, go. I know you have to go. He's your best friend. Go."

He puts his hands on my shoulders and looks at me, but I can already tell his mind is somewhere else. "This . . . we can't do this right now. This isn't the story I want to tell our grandkids about how we got engaged."

"I know," I whisper. "I know. Go. We can talk about it when you get back."

He hugs me and buries his face in my hair. "I told Mack I wouldn't let you out of my sight."

"Amar and Amina are in custody. And this is Rome. It's safe. I've traveled all over the world by myself. I'll be fine." I pause for a second as he squeezes me tighter. "I'm so sorry about JJ. You have to go. Get the people who did this."

"Mason," Hawk says, pointing to Butch who's standing outside a van that's just come to a screeching halt in front of the piazza. "We've got to go."

Mason leans over and gives me one last soft kiss. "I love you. I'm the luckiest person alive."

"Nope," I say, trying to smile. "I'm the luckiest."

He starts walking backward to the van. "We can decide later who's the luckiest." He's trying to smile, too. "I'll call you from the plane."

We watch each other until he hesitantly closes the van door. After the van speeds off, I hear the little girl laughing behind me. I turn around to see her mother tickling her nose with a daisy she's plucked from the flower bed next to them. I watch them play for a second before I collapse back onto the bench—sobbing so hard I can barely catch my breath.

Chapter Twenty-Nine

MASON, IN-FLIGHT, ROME TO JALALABAD, 2020

"What's wrong?" Mack answers on the first ring. "Is Millie okay?"

"She's fine. The job's done. She can fill you in on the details, but she's fine." I take a deep breath. "JJ's dead."

"How?" It's the first question we ask. So many of our brothers have died in service that we don't even feign surprise anymore.

"On a mission. I can't get into details right now." I pause for a second. He doesn't say anything. He knows. "Mack, I've got to track down the people who killed him. I'm already on a plane headed to Afghanistan."

"I know. Do what you need to do."

"I promised you I wouldn't leave Millie alone. I left her in Rome—"

"Millie will be fine," he says. "I've got her until you get back. Take care of business and get home to her."

"I just tried to call her. She didn't answer. Will you try?"

"Mason, she's a grown woman. It took me a while to realize that, but she is. She'll be fine, but yeah, I'll call her when we get off."

"There's something else." I hesitate. "She doesn't want me to tell you, but if something happens to me I want you to know—"

"Nothing's going to happen to you."

"That day at the barbecue when the agency director showed up—he told Millie that Amar Petrovic might be her father. He married her mom right before she died. Millie didn't want to tell you. She just talked to Amar, he confirmed they got married, but he kept ignoring her when she insisted he wasn't her father. She's never thought he was, but I want you to know. Millie keeps things from people so—"

"Mason," he says quietly. "I know what she does. She doesn't want to hurt the people she loves. She's my daughter. She knows that as well as I do, but I'll talk to her about it. Thanks for telling me. Just get home safely."

"There's more Mack." I'm not sure I should tell him, but I know I'd want to know. "Nejra sent you a letter to tell you about the baby. She gave it to Amar to mail. He burned it. He said he told her that before she died, so she knew you didn't get it. I'm sure she knew you would have come for her."

Mack takes a long, loud breath. "She knew I would come for her," he says finally. "She knew. Did he tell you any more about how she died?"

"Yeah, peacefully. Haroun Hadzic's wife drugged her when she realized what her husband was going to do. Nejra was sleeping when he smothered her. Amar saw it happen. She didn't struggle. She never woke up. Millie was sleeping on her chest at the time and didn't wake up either, so it must have been very peaceful."

"Does Millie know all this?" His voice is starting to get angry.

"Yeah. When I left, she seemed okay, but I know she's not. She needs you."

"I'll call her right now."

"God, I shouldn't have left her," I say, blowing a breath out through my teeth. "I'm sorry, Mack."

"Son, you listen to me and you listen good," he says, his voice getting deeper. "Get your head in the game. Millie's fine. I'm fine. Worry about yourself and your team. That's it. If you don't, you're going to come back in a body bag, too. Get over there, do your damn job, and then get back to my daughter. You understand me?"

"Yes, sir."

"Mason, she needs you every bit as much as she needs me. We're a team now. Get this done and get your ass back here."

As I hang up with Mack, Culver's making his way across the plane to me.

"We got some more information on JJ," he says. "I'm not sure you want to hear it."

"I probably need to though," I say, sighing. "Just tell me."

"The coroner did tests on him. He had heavy levels of meth in his system."

"What?" I say, shaking my head to try to make sense of what he said. "JJ never took drugs. You know that. His body was a temple. He was healthier than any of us."

"Yeah, I know. The coroner said he didn't have any signs of long-term use. It must have been just recently that he started using. You know how agitated he's been these last couple of months. I thought it was stress, but apparently, it was more."

I lean over and put my head in my hands. "Why didn't he tell me? God, this is my fault."

"Mason, it's not your fault. I know I don't need to tell you that." He pats me on the back. "You know some of our guys are using to help them stay energized. We're trying to eliminate it, but it's there."

I sit up quickly. "No one on my team was or is using. No one. I don't know how he hid it from me."

"He didn't hide it from you. I don't think he was using when you were here. By the time he started, you were out in San Diego. There's no way you could have known."

"Maybe I shouldn't have left—"

"Mason, I know there's not a brain cell in your head that believes that," he says. "You know you made the right decision."

"Yeah, for me, but not for him."

"Everybody's got to do what's right for himself. If you had stayed with the team, you would have been thinking about Millie all the time. You know you wouldn't have been happy. You made the right decision for you. That's all that matters. JJ needed to figure it out. He just chose the wrong way."

"But he seemed fine in Pakistan," I say, squinting as I try to remember it clearly. "He was focused, calm. It's just been these last few weeks that he's been all over the place. I should have listened to you. He wasn't ready for the lead."

"Look, JJ was one of the finest operators to ever wear the uniform," Culver says. "I wouldn't have appointed him at lead if I didn't think he was capable. It was more than that—the divorce, the team breaking up. Some people can handle a full on firefight better than they can handle change. I think he was one of those people. Best thing we can do now is get over there and find the people who did this. Get your head in the game. We owe this to him."

Chapter Thirty

Mason's called me three times in the ten minutes he's been gone. I haven't answered because I don't want him to hear me crying. I'm still sitting on the bench in the piazza when my phone rings again. It's Dad. I pick it up quickly. I need to hear his voice so badly right now.

"Dad?" I say as the tears start streaming down my face again.

"Sweetie," he says softly. "You're okay. Everything's okay. Mason called me. He told me about Amar. He's not your dad, Mills. You know that—"

"I know." I'm sobbing again. I can barely get the words out. "I n-never thought he was."

"Millie. Honey, where are you right now? Are you safe?"

"Y-yes." I sniff loudly into the phone as I try to wipe some of the tears off my face. "I'm still in Rome. I'm sitting in a piazza. JJ died. Mason had to leave—"

"I talked to him. I know about everything. I need you to get home right now. Okay? Can you leave?"

"I think so." My voice stops shaking a little bit. I honestly forgot I could leave. I guess my job's done. I need to get back to Dad.

"Okay, why don't I stay on the phone with you while you walk back to the hotel?"

As I stand up, I see Amina Petrovic rushing across the piazza toward me.

"Millie?" Dad says. "Are you still there?"

"Dad, I have to call you back."

"Where is he?" Amina screams. She's changed out of her tea-stained white dress and is now wearing a very wrinkled cotton shirt with jeans. She looks every bit as disheveled as she did the first time I met her in Sarajevo.

"Millie, what's wrong? Who is that?" Dad yells.

"Dad, patch Raine into this call—"

"Millie!"

"Dad, just do it, please. I'll leave the line open, but I can't talk anymore right now." I slip the phone into my shirt pocket.

"Amina," I say. "What are you doing here?"

"Amar must have finally put the battery back in his phone. I tracked it and arrived at the villa just in time to see you leaving with one of your protectors, but he's left. It's just us now. Where is my husband?"

She has her hand inside her crossbody bag. I'm guessing it's holding a gun.

"Amina, you're being followed." I sit back down on the bench. "Don't take the gun out. They'll shoot you."

"No one is following me." She takes a step closer to me, her hand still in the bag. "I would have noticed."

"I don't think you would have. They're pretty good at being invisible."

"Where is my husband?" Her voice lowers into a growl, but it's shaking. She at least half-believes that someone's watching us. I'm guessing by this time Raine has called it in. I haven't heard anything from my phone since Raine initially got on the line. I hope she's still listening.

"Amar's in custody. The authorities have already taken him away."

She starts shifting nervously. I can almost see the wheels turning in her head. "Did he give it to you? Where is it?"

"Amar didn't give anything to me."

"Then who did he give it to?" Her hand gets more active in the bag.

I smile. "If you mean the flash drive that contains all your communication with Sayid, he gave that to the authorities. Your time's up, Amina."

The news makes her hesitate like I knew it would. As she double-clutches her grip on the gun, I jump up and land a right hook squarely between the top of her cheek and her temple— just like Dad taught me. She crumples to the ground.

"Millie! Back up!" I look up to see our agent Brad following some Italian SWAT into the piazza. They slowly circle us.

I raise my hands as I back up. Brad leans over Amina and checks her pulse.

"She's alive," he says, looking up at me, "but damn, you knocked her clean out."

He stands up and reaches his arm out for a high five.

"How did you lose her? She almost killed me, you asshole," I say, slapping his arm away as I take my cell phone out of my pocket.

"Dad?"

"Millie, oh my God, sweetie." He lets out a huge breath. "What happened? Are you okay? Are you safe? Who's this guy you're talking to? Put me on the phone with him right now. Is he responsible for this?"

"Dad, I'm fine. It was Amar's wife. She was involved in Sayid's network. She had a gun. I knocked her out. I'm fine. I'll explain later. Stay on the phone with me, okay?" I swat Brad's hands away again as he tries to help me toward the waiting car.

Brad opens the car door. "Let's get back to the villa. The director's jet is waiting for you when you're ready, but I guess it'll just be you since Raine's headed to Jbad with the team. I can fly home with you if you want company."

"Hard pass," I say, scowling at him as I block him from getting in the back with me. "You're in the front with the driver. Raine, are you still on the phone?"

"Yeah, Mills," she says. "You okay?"

"I'm fine. Did you hear everything?"

"Yeah, I'm on it. I'll find out who's responsible for losing her."

"I didn't know you went with the team. I thought you were still here. Maybe don't tell Mason about this for now."

"Tell him about what?" she says, laughing. "I'm hanging up now. I'll call you later."

I hear her line drop. "Dad?"

"Millie, what the fuck?"

"It's my job, Dad," I say. "It happens sometimes."

"You could have died—"

"No, not this time. She wasn't any match for me. Someone taught me how to defend myself at a very young age."

"I taught you self-defense to fight off asshole men," he says sternly. "Not to defend yourself against armed terrorists."

"Well, you'll be happy to know it works on both," I say as the car pulls up in front of the villa. "Hey, Dad, I need to get cleaned up and pack. I'll call you when I get on the plane. Will you pick me up at the base when we land?"

"I'm headed there now—"

"Dad," I say, smiling. "We won't arrive until tomorrow morning."

"On time is late, Mills." He pauses for a second. "Just get back here, okay? I'll be waiting."

Chapter Thirty-One

"You want the good news or bad news first?" Raine says as she sits down on the bench next to me.

"How about you just give me the news?" I snarl. I've been in the worst mood since I left Millie in that plaza. She hasn't answered my calls, and now Mack's not picking up either.

"Okay," Raine says as she scoots back from me a bit.

"I'm sorry, Raine. I'm in a bad mood, but I shouldn't take it out on you. Bad news first."

"We lost the rest of the guys that killed JJ. They disappeared back up into the mountains. We'll find them, but it could take a while. So it looks like we're going to be in a holding pattern for a while."

"A holding pattern in Jbad or Virginia?"

"Not my call, but we're landing in Jalalabad, so I imagine we'll be there for the night at least."

I take a deep breath trying to keep calm. "Okay, now give me the good news."

"Millie's not Amar's daughter. Not even a small chance." Raine pauses for a second as she tries to read my expression. "Are you going to tell her?"

"I don't know," I say, turning my head to her. "Are you?"

"No, this is between you and her. I was following orders."

I nod. "If I tell her, I promise I won't let on that you helped me."

"Mason," she says, looking down. "Millie's smarter than both of us combined. She'll know who helped you. I'm okay with that. Tell her if you want to."

"Wait, you're not looking at me. What aren't you telling me?"

"What? Nothing!" She tries to look up at me but looks down again quickly.

"Raine, you're not as good a liar as Millie is—"

"Well that sucks for you considering what you just had me do," she says, standing up. "Talk to Millie. You two give me a headache. I'll keep you updated on the JJ stuff."

"Raine—"

Ty comes over as Raine walks away. I want to finish my conversation with her, but it will wait. She's never been able to keep information from me.

"Culver told me about JJ's test results," Ty says as he sits down. "I suspected he was using. I should have told you. JJ could still be alive today if I had."

"C'mon, Ty," I say, patting him on the shoulder. "You know the only guy who's responsible for JJ's death is the guy who pulled the trigger."

"Yeah, I do know that." He locks his eyes with mine. "Do you?'

I shake my head and laugh. "Turning my words against me, huh? You've always been the smartest guy on this team."

"Not much of a competition," he says, smiling. "It's not your fault, Mase, any more than it's mine. JJ made his own decisions."

"Yeah, I wish I would have been there to protect him though."

"He'd smack you on the side of the head if he heard you say that," Ty laughs. "JJ never needed anyone to protect him."

"And after he smacked me, he'd remind me that he's a better shot than me, so he'd be the one protecting me." I smile, nodding my head. "He never let me forget that."

"He was a good guy, Mase, who made some bad decisions in the end. Best we can hope for is to get the guys responsible. You know how this works."

"Yeah," I say, leaning my head back and closing my eyes.

"Hey, I talked to Culver about taking over the team. He supports it. I hope you do, too."

I sit back up quickly. Ty's always so quiet. I hadn't thought about him in the lead. I look at him for a minute and then nod my head.

"Yeah, you know what? I do support that. I think you'd be great."

"Thanks, Mase. That means a lot to me. Culver's going to get me started when we get back. He told me about Butch and Hawk retiring. It's a loss for sure, but I think it's going to be good for me to get a new team. You know? Fresh start for everyone."

"I completely agree with that. Damn, Ty, I'm sorry I didn't think about this sooner. You'll be great."

"Naw, there's no need to be sorry. I wasn't ready for it until now. Sometimes you have to wait for something to slap you in the face before you know you're ready for it."

When he says that, it makes me think of Millie. I was hesitant when she said she was finally ready to marry me. I want her to be sure, but maybe it happened that way for her—maybe it just slapped her in the face all of a sudden.

"Mase? Are you second-guessing me?" Ty's looking at me, concerned. "I think the timing's right. I know it is."

"Damn sure, it's right." I chuck him on the shoulder. "I'm proud of you, brother."

Raine walks back over and hands me the satellite phone. "It's Millie."

I leap up and grab it out of her hands. "Babe? I've been trying to call you—"

"I know, Mase." She sighs. "I'm sorry. I just got off the phone with Dad. Then Paul Ward called me."

"Are you okay? Are you still in Rome?"

"I'm on the plane—headed home. Where are you?"

"We're about an hour from landing."

"Do they have the targets locked?" I can't believe how steady her voice sounds. It makes me feel a little better.

"No, they lost them," I say. "We might turn right back around if they don't find them in the next few hours."

"I'm sorry, Mase. I know you want to find them."

"We'll find them eventually." I sit back down on the bench and close my eyes. "Did you say you talked to the director? What did he want?"

"He wants to hire me full-time as a consultant."

"What? Seriously?"

"Yeah," she says, laughing. "And, he wants you, Butch, and Hawk to work with me with Raine as our agency handler."

"Wow," I say, trying to process the information. "What did you tell him?"

"I told him no but he said he's going to keep after me."

"If he shows up at our house again, I'm going to be pissed."

"I don't think he will, but he'll probably bug us for a while." She pauses and then whispers, "Mase, you can't believe how much money he deposited into my account for this job. I don't want to say how much over the phone, but it's insane for two days work."

"You're worth every penny of whatever it is, but he's probably trying to sway your decision, too."

"Yeah, I know. That's not going to work. I don't need his money. I still have some of Camille's inheritance, but I guess I'm going to have to find a job when we get back."

"We'll have my retirement after I get out next year. We'll be fine. You don't have to do anything you don't want to do."

Raine's been glancing over at me since she handed me the phone. She's trying to figure out if Millie's told me whatever they're hiding from me.

"More importantly right now, why don't you tell me what Raine's hiding from me? She won't look at me."

Millie sighs. "God, she's an awful liar—"

"The worst," I say, laughing. "She's going to tell me if you don't. You know I'll force it out of her."

"Yeah," she says slowly. "Don't overreact. Okay?"

"That doesn't make me feel any better."

"Look, long story, short. After you left the piazza, Amina Petrovic showed up. She had a gun. I knocked her out. The authorities finally got there and arrested her. She's gone."

I take a deep breath and blow it out. "Okay. I feel like you're leaving out huge, important chunks of that story—"

"I'm fine."

"That's the most important thing, but we're going to get way more into that story when I get home." I pause for a second. "For instance, what do you mean when you say you knocked her out?"

"Knocked her out cold with a right hook. One shot and she was down."

I try unsuccessfully to suppress a laugh. "Okay, killer. I guess you really are Mack's daughter. That's his favorite punch, too."

"Speaking of," she says. "Why don't you tell me what Raine won't tell me about you? You know I can get stuff out of her, too."

"With the right hook?"

"If necessary," she says. "Stop stalling, Mason. Confess. What did you do?"

"You're going to be pissed."

"Just tell me—"

"I tested your blood against Amar's," I blurt out.

"I know," she says, laughing. "I saw you steal the Kleenex. You're not as sneaky as you think you are."

"Why didn't you tell me you saw me? Are you mad?"

"No, I know it's just who you are." She sighs, but I can tell she's not mad. "Did Raine test it for you?"

"Yeah, but don't be mad at her, babe. She didn't want to. I was kind of an asshole to her about it."

"I'm not mad at anyone."

"You're not Amar's daughter. Not even a little bit of a chance."

"I never thought I was." She pauses for a second. "I'm not mad at you. I know you were trying to protect me like you always do."

"Someone has to—"

"Umm, you know, I took care of two armed people in the last day without you."

My heart stops beating for a second. "Are you trying to kill me right now, Millie? Because if you are, good job. I already feel so guilty."

"Mase." She has that little growl in her voice that she gets when she's trying to settle me down. "I'm just teasing you. I didn't mean it like that. It's just, I can take care of myself if I need to—"

"Baby, I know you can. I've known that from the beginning. But I don't want you to. That's my job and it makes me crazy when I'm not there to do it."

"I know, babe. And honestly, I don't want to take care of myself anymore. You do it so much better."

"I want to be with you so badly right now." I shake my head to try to clear the frustration I'm feeling. "After we get the people who killed JJ, I think I can go back to San Diego. We can get back to our normal life. Okay?"

"Okay." She lets out a long yawn. "Mase, I'm exhausted. I'm going to try to get some sleep."

"Okay, baby," I whisper. "Do you want me to stay on the phone while you fall asleep?"

"Yes. Do you have time?"

"All the time in the world. Close your eyes. I won't hang up until you're asleep."

When I hear her breathing become slow and steady, I reluctantly disconnect the phone. All I can think about is how mad I am that I'm not curled up behind her, spooning her as she sleeps.

Chapter Thirty-Two

SARAJEVO, BOSNIA, 1995

"Sayid, you know the baby would be better off with me," Azayiz said to her nephew. "Please let me take her to Pakistan."

Sayid shook his head as he hugged Yasmine tighter. "She's all I have left of Nejra—of my family. She has to stay with me."

Azayiz walked over to him and placed her hand gently on his shoulder. "I know how much you miss Nejra. I miss her, too, but we have to think of what is best for Yasmine. You have to work. I will be able to stay home with her. Or maybe you can move to Pakistan with Fareed and me. We can be a family there."

Sayid shook his head as the tears started falling down his face again. He knew she was right, but he couldn't imagine giving up the only piece of his family he had left. Yasmine's eyes were starting to turn green, just like Nejra's. That made him feel connected to her despite her fair skin and the red hair that was becoming more prominent.

"Do you want to tell me again who impregnated Nejra?" Sayid hissed. "I know you know who it was, and it certainly wasn't anyone who lives in this town. It happened at that job, didn't it? I knew she lied to me about who she was working for."

"She was raped, walking home—"

"Stop!" Sayid yelled, causing Yasmine to start crying again. Sayid pointed at her head. "Where does she get this skin and this hair? It can only be from a Westerner. Was she working with Americans? I heard they were in town—trying to bring the war to an end. Did one of them rape her? I can't even leave the house without covering the baby up completely. They already want me to kill her. If they saw her, they would want that even more."

"She is my daughter," Amar said, walking over from the corner of the room. "I was married to Nejra. I want to take her to Italy as we planned. She will blend in better there."

"You know as well as I do Nejra didn't want to marry you," Sayid said with the biting anger that had taken over his mind since Nejra died. "Yasmine is not your baby and you are not taking her."

Amar took a step toward him but backed up quickly when Sayid glared up at him. He had never seen anything close to this kind of anger from Sayid.

"Sayid," Azayiz said. "You are squeezing the baby too hard. That's why she's crying. Please let me hold her."

Sayid loosened his grip on Yasmine but turned away from Azayiz's outstretched arms. "I want you both to leave."

Sayid moved out of Azayiz's house two weeks after Nejra died and took the baby with him. He was living in a shabby one-room apartment. Azayiz visited every day to make sure he was taking care of Yasmine. She feared that he would kill the baby, but it had been almost three months and he hadn't yet.

"I brought you more diapers and baby formula," Azayiz said. "You need to feed her more often. She's not gaining enough weight."

"Leave," Sayid said. "Yasmine is my responsibility."

As Azayiz and Amar walked out of the apartment building, Azayiz stopped and looked up at Amar.

"We have to contact him—"

"No," Amar said, shaking his head.

"We were wrong not to send her letter. We have to contact him now. It's the only way we can get the baby away from Sayid. She's not safe with him."

"He won't come. He was using Nejra for sex. He won't want anything to do with the baby."

"We have to try," Azayiz said. "I have American contacts in Pakistan. I will try to get his phone number from them. You need to place the call. He will take it more seriously coming from a man."

"No, I won't do it."

"Amar, do you want Yasmine to die?" Azayiz paused and looked up at the sky. "You owe this to Nejra. We both do. It's the only way."

As Mack approached the door, he could hear the baby howling. He quickly picked the lock and found her lying on a blanket in the middle of the dark one-bedroom apartment. It was stifling hot in the room. Mack looked around quickly and put his gun back in his waistband.

As he bent over and picked up her sweaty body, he smiled as he saw the red hair that he'd seen through his binoculars the day before.

"Hey there," he whispered. "I like your hair. It looks just like mine."

The baby rubbed her eyes as she tried to focus on him. She whimpered as she looked up at him.

"Do you have a name?" Mack said, smiling at her. "We'll have to figure that out. Shh. It's okay, sweetie. I'm not going to let anything bad happen to you ever again. I bet you're hungry, but we have to wait until we get out of town. Okay? This will all be over soon."

Mack closed his eyes and took a deep breath as the baby laid her head on his shoulder. He turned around and walked out the door. When he saw a man approaching him, he lowered his baseball cap and held the baby's head tightly to his chest. The man passed without even looking at him. Two more people passed him as he left the building. They barely noticed him. He kept his head down until he got to his car.

Mack put the baby into the car seat that the woman at the rental car agency in Budapest showed him how to use. He told her that his sister had died in childbirth and that he was the baby's only living relative. After she heard that, she spent an hour with him outlining everything he needed for the baby.

She told him exactly what he needed and where he could buy it in Budapest.

After he left her, he filled his trunk with baby supplies—diapers, formula, pacifiers, blankets, baby wipes—before he started the long drive to Bosnia. He mixed several bottles of formula yesterday and iced them down in a cooler he bought. He was more prepared for this mission than he had been for any other in his career. He had no idea SEAL training would be so useful for baby preparation.

As he started the car, he looked back at the baby. "We have a long drive ahead of us, sweetie. I'll stop when we get out of town to feed and change you."

Mack laughed at himself, knowing the baby couldn't understand what he was saying, but she stopped crying every time he talked. He told her all about Nejra until he couldn't hear her whimpering anymore. After he was sure she was asleep, he called Chase.

"I've got her," he said as Chase answered.

Chase took a deep breath. "Are you sure she's yours?"

"Not a doubt in my mind."

"Where are you? Is the Sarajevo airport still closed?"

"Yeah, I'm driving back to Budapest."

"That's a long drive—"

"She'll be fine."

"I'm more worried about you. Do you even know how to change a diaper?"

"Did you how to when you had Sammi?"

"No, but I had Mariel and grandmas and aunts—"

"I'll figure it out. It can't be that hard. I didn't know how to shoot a rifle before I joined the Navy, but I'm an expert at it now."

"That's debatable," Chase said, laughing. "Mack, are you sure about this?"

"Yeah, the second I looked at her."

He sighed. "Okay, brother. Just get her home. We'll figure it out together. I've got your cell tracked, but still call me when you get to the airport in Budapest. Tell me what airport you're flying into here. I'll pick you up."

Mack was almost to the Croatian border before the baby woke up. He pulled over when she started crying.

"All right, first things first," he said as he closed the trunk and climbed into the back seat with her. "Let's get your diaper changed. Uncle Chase doesn't think we can do it, but it can't be that hard, right?"

The baby looked up at him and cooed when he started talking. He kept talking as he attempted to change her diaper several times. He held her up after he fastened the tape on the third diaper. It stayed in place and she smiled at him, so he figured he had it right.

"We did good. Okay, now clothes," he said, reaching into the baby bag. "These are called onesies. I didn't know such a thing existed until last week. I'm sure I'm going to learn a lot of new things with you. And I have the little footed pajamas for you. Those are the best. I had some when I was little."

He laughed as she pumped her arms and legs in the air. "You're a wiggly, little thing, aren't you? You're making it hard to get this on. Are you always going to be this stubborn? I'm guessing by the look in your eyes you are. I'm stubborn, and I think your mom was, so it makes sense that you would be, too. I hope you look like her when you grow up because she was beautiful. You have her eyes, but I think you're going to have my hair."

Mack finally got her dressed and grabbed one of the bottles out of the cooler. He snuggled her to his chest as she greedily sucked on the bottle. "Big appetite, too, huh? Yeah, you're definitely my kid."

After she finished, he burped her as the rental car woman had instructed him, and rocked her until she fell back asleep. As he put her back in the car seat, he tried to remember the car rental woman's name. She said it was French.

"Millicent," he said out loud. "It was Millicent."

He looked at the baby, peacefully sleeping next to him. "Yep, that's it. Your name is Millicent, but I think I'm going to call you Millie. Is that okay with you? It is? Okay, it's settled then."

He smiled as he walked to the driver's door. Before he got in the car, he looked up at the sky. "Did you name her? I hope you don't mind if I change it. I'll take such good care of her. I promise. Nothing's more important to me from this day forward. Rest easy, Nejra. I've got her now."

Chapter Thirty-Three

MILLIE, VIRGINIA BEACH, VIRGINIA, 2020

When I get off the plane, I walk directly to the visitor's lot. Dad's leaning against his car. I drop my bag and run to him. I'm surprised I don't knock him over when I crash into his arms. My arms wrap around his neck tightly as he pulls me to him.

"I never stopped being your dad," he whispers. "No matter what anyone said. I've been your dad from the very beginning."

"I know." I'm crying again. My hormones are so whacked out. I'm like a week late for my period, too, and that rarely happens.

"I've got something I want to show you," he says, kissing my forehead before he reaches into his car and pulls out some papers. "It's the paternity test I did on you when you were a baby."

"Dad," I say, taking a step back. "I don't need to see that."

"I know you don't need to, but I want you to look at it anyway."

"No," I say, swatting the paper away from me. "How do you even still have those results? Chase told me after he thought you died, he got rid of most of your stuff."

"I always carried this with me in my wallet—even on missions. It never left me. That's why it's so torn up."

"Why did you carry it?" I say, narrowing my eyes. "So you could prove I belonged to you?"

"No. No one ever asked that. It's just—" he says and then stops for a minute, looking down. "You know, I wasn't there when you were born. And even though I knew you were mine from the second I saw you, getting these results was like you being born for me. I don't know. When I look at this piece of paper, I guess I feel like some people feel when they look at those pictures of their baby when it's still in the mom—"

"A sonogram?"

"Yeah, that. That's what this piece of paper feels like to me. Does that make sense?"

I nod, smiling at him. "Yeah, but I told you, I don't need proof. I know I'm yours."

"Millie, it's important to me that you see the results—"

"But I don't need to, Dad."

"Sweetie, do you remember what I used to do back in the day when you didn't want to do your homework?" Dad raises his eyebrows, smiling slightly like he always did right before he launched a surprise attack on me when I was growing up.

I take a step back. "Uh, you would bribe me with strawberry ice cream?" I say hopefully.

"Not that one." He takes a step toward me. "The more direct method I used."

"Yeah." I laugh as I take another step back. "You would put me in a headlock and force me to study."

"I did not put you in a headlock. I merely put my arm around you while I lovingly encouraged you to complete your assignments."

I roll my eyes. "So, what? If I don't look at the results, you're going to put me in a headlock and force me? You know I'm a lot stronger than I used to be."

"Still the same amount of stubborn though," he says, grinning at me as he leans back against the car. He motions for me to join him. "Why don't you do this without a fight so you won't hurt your old dad?"

"Fine," I say with all the drama I can muster as I lean next to him.

He opens up the test results and points to the line that reads "The probability of paternity is 99.9999%."

I look up at him. "Well there's still a .0001 chance that I don't belong to you, so we might as well say goodbye now."

He grabs me into a gentle headlock. "Nope, there's not a chance you got that sarcasm from anyone but me."

I take a deep breath as I relax onto his chest. "When you first saw the results, were you happy?"

"I knew you were my daughter the first time I saw you. The test was just a formality."

"No, but I mean, you weren't expecting to hear you had a baby. Was the test being positive a good thing?"

He wraps both of his big arms around me and pulls me tightly to his chest. "Sweetie, you are, and will always be, the best thing that ever happened in my life. And I know, even for that short time, you were the best thing that ever happened to Nejra, too."

I lift my head from his chest and look at him. "That's the first time you've ever called Mom by her first name. I mean, to me anyway."

"Yeah, I've been thinking," he says. His eyes start to twinkle. "If it's okay with you, I'd like to start talking about Nejra a little more. She and I spent a lot of time talking. I want to tell you some of the things she told me and tell you a little bit more about her in general. She was so special. I still miss her sometimes."

I nod my head as the tears start to pour down my face more steadily. "I'd like that, Dad. I want to hear everything."

He tightens his arms around me. "And I thought maybe we could contact that woman we met at your aunt's funeral. I think she said she was Nejra's second cousin. She said she had a lot of pictures of Nejra. Do you want some of those?"

"Yeah," I say, sniffling. "When I have kids one day, I want to show them their grandma."

Dad reaches up and wipes my face with his hands including my runny nose.

"Ooo, Dad, don't wipe my snot with your hands."

"Do you know how many times I've wiped snot off your face? Not to mention all the times I wiped your butt," he says, laughing. "Did I ever tell you about the first time I tried to change your diaper?"

"No," I say, smiling as his face lights up. "You haven't told me anything."

He laughs, shaking his head. "It took me three times to get

it right and even then it was pretty shaky. We were in the back seat of a rental car on our way from Sarajevo to Budapest. God, I'm so glad I flew into Budapest. This woman at the rental car agency helped me when I told her I was there to take you home. She made lists of what I needed and made sure I got a car with a baby seat. That's who you're named after, by the way. Did I tell you that?'

"What? No!" I can't quit laughing at him. I don't think I've ever seen him this happy. "I'm named after a rental car lady?"

"She went by Millicent, but yeah, I would have been completely lost if she hadn't helped me. I was pretty lost anyway. Those first couple days, I was scared, but every time I looked at you or talked to you, you would smile so big and quit crying immediately."

"I still do that." I lay my head back down on his chest. "Tell me something about Mom right now."

"She was sweet and funny and smart, and she knew exactly what she wanted. And I know she wanted you with everything in her because she had an enormous heart." He pauses for a second. "Is that enough for now?"

"One more thing."

"She told me her dad was much too tolerant of his head-strong daughter," he says, messing up my hair. "Remind you of anyone?"

"Yeah," I say, smiling as I look up at him. "Was she always hungry, too?"

"Nope, that you get from me." He leads me around to the passenger's side. "You want to get lunch?"

"Yeah, maybe tacos?"

"Yeah, sweetie, anything you want," he says, kissing my forehead, "and then probably ice cream for dessert."

Chapter Thirty-Four

We're headed back home after only spending one night in Afghanistan. The agency still hasn't located the rest of the people responsible for JJ's death. Until they do, we don't have much of a reason to be there. I'm angry, frustrated, and grumpy. Not only because we lost the trail of JJ's killers, but also because I don't want to be here. In my almost twenty years of service, I've never felt this way. I've loved this job, but I feel like it's done for me now.

"Hey," Culver says, snapping me out of my thoughts. "Did Ty tell you he's taking over the team?"

"Yeah," I say, nodding. "I think it's great. He's solid."

"Yeah, I do, too. I'm glad he stepped up." He sits down next to me. "It's going to take him a while to get up to speed. But even after he's there, I'm not sending you back to California, Mason. I know you don't want to hear that, but I need you in Virginia Beach. I told you when you came back that you were in it for a while."

I take a deep breath and nod. From the look in Culver's eyes, I'm not doing a good job of keeping the anger I'm feeling hidden.

"I know you want to get back to San Diego, but it's my job to do what's best for the teams. You being active is what's best. You're the best operator we have. We need you." He pauses for me to reply. I don't. "Are you going to retire at twenty?"

"Yes," I hiss.

"Well, it's only a year. Maybe Millie can stay in Virginia."

As he gets up to walk away, my mind starts spinning. I can't ask Millie to stay in Virginia when I'm going to be on missions ninety percent of the time. Even if Mack stays with her, I don't want her waiting for me to come home—not knowing if I'm going to get back alive. I'm going to have to convince her to go back to California without me for her own good.

My other option is to retire right now. If I do that, I'll lose a lot of the pension that I'll get if I stick it out for another year. That doesn't make any sense. It's only a year. So why does it feel like it's going to be another twenty?

I grab the satellite phone and call Millie. She's laughing when she answers.

"Hey," I say. "Where are you?"

"Hey! I'm with Dad. Are you still in Afghanistan?"

"No, we're headed back—"

"Oh, Mase, we just got to the Outer Banks, but we can turn around, so I can pick you up when you land."

"No, babe, don't," I say. "We might be right back out if they find them."

"Are you okay? You don't sound very good."

"I'm just frustrated." I change the subject. "I didn't know you were going to the Outer Banks."

"Yeah, we decided to come down here to surf one more time before we all head back to California."

I try to make my voice work, but I don't want to tell her.

"Mase, what's wrong?"

"Culver's not letting me go back to California. I'm going to be in Virginia—and active—until I can retire next year."

I hear her take a deep breath. "Mase, I mean, that sucks, but we can figure it out. I'll stay in Virginia with you. It's only a year."

"No, I don't want you there. It's no life for you even if Mack stays. I'm never going to be home. And when I'm active, I'm not easy to be around. It's just going to be different. You need to go back to California."

"Why don't I come back to Virginia Beach right now?" She's whispering. I'm guessing Mack's sitting next to her. "We can talk about it. What time do you land?"

"Millie, I love you, but I don't want to talk about it right now, okay? I'm mad and frustrated. I need some time to sort this out in my head. Stay down there with Mack and enjoy yourself. We can talk about it when you get back."

She doesn't say anything for a minute. "Okay. We planned to be down here for two days. We're going to spend some time with Carol. She and Dad are kind of together again, I guess. But, I can come back—"

"No, baby," I say. "That sounds fun. Enjoy yourself. We can talk when you get back here."

"Okay. Will you call me when you land?"

"Yeah."

When I hang up, I can tell from her voice that I've ruined her day. It's the last thing I wanted to do. All I want to do is make her happy—every second of every day. That's what I want to do with the rest of my life and I want that life to start now.

Chapter Thirty-Five

MILLIE, OUTER BANKS, NORTH CAROLINA, 2020

"Dad," I say as I knock on his hotel room door.

We got to the Outer Banks last night and had dinner with Carol. I left them at the hotel bar at about nine. He was supposed to meet me this morning at eight to go surfing. It's fifteen minutes after eight. For him, that's the equivalent of being an entire week late.

Mariel told me that Carol spent the night with him in Virginia Beach while I was in Rome. From the way they were looking at each other last night, I'm guessing that's why he's late this morning. As much as I love the idea of them being together, I don't want to open this door to see them in bed.

Dad swings the door open. "Hey! Sorry, running a little late this morning."

He's putting the finishing touches on making his bed. He always has his bed made by five in the morning.

"Is she hiding in the bathroom?" I nod my head toward the closed door as I fold my arms over my chest.

"Who, sweetie?" He avoids eye contact with me.

"Dad," I say, rolling my eyes. "I'm a trained CIA interrogator now. Stop trying to fool me. I know Carol spent the night with you while I was in Rome. She doesn't have to hide from me. I love her."

"She left about ten minutes ago," he says, finally looking at me. "Thank God Chase and Mariel already left for Colorado, so I don't have to kill Mariel when we get back. She shouldn't have told you that."

"It's not Mariel's fault," I say, laughing. "You're the one hiding stuff."

He sits on the bed. "It's just, you know, with everything you just heard about Nejra, I don't want to give you too much to handle all at once."

"Dad." I sit next to him. "Carol's a good thing—for me anyway. Is she a good thing for you?"

"Yeah, she is." He puts his arm around me as I lay my head on his shoulder. "She's considering moving out to San Diego."

"Really? Her entire family's here." I look up at him. "If you want to stay here with her, I'll understand."

"I've already told her that's not a possibility. You're the most important thing to me. She gets that."

"But—"

"Millie, it's not an option. As long as you want me to, I'm going to live in the same city as you. If you get tired of me, I'll consider moving, but I probably wouldn't even then. You're stuck with me."

"I'm never going to get tired of you."

"Good, then it's settled." He stands up and pulls me up

with him. "Let's get to the beach. There's supposed to be some good waves out today."

Dad and I have just paddled out. He told me to go first, but I motioned him into the next wave. It's choppy out and it's giving me motion sickness. I haven't had that once in my entire life. I watch him ride the wave for a while but then decide to paddle in—despite the growing dizziness in my head.

The second I pop up on my board, my head starts spinning like a top. I feel myself falling and can't stop it. My legs go up in the air as my head crashes back down on the board. I make it back to the surface, but my head's pounding.

"Wow! That was a spectacular wipeout! I think you just handed the surfing crown back to me." Dad laughs as he paddles his board over.

I look up at him as he glides in next to me. "I don't know what happened—"

"I do," he says, grinning. "You lost it on a baby wave. I haven't seen you wipe out on something that little since you were about six."

I try to smile, but tears start rolling down my cheeks. I go under water to try to wash them away before he can see them.

"Millie?" As I surface, he takes my arms and drapes them over his board. "What's wrong? Did you hit your head?"

I nod as the tears start to stream down my face. He reaches down and pulls me up onto his board.

"Look at me," he says, grabbing my face. "Look right into my eyes."

I try to, but my head's still spinning. The more it spins, the harder I cry.

"Okay, sweetie," he says as he slides off the board. "Lie down. I'll paddle us in. We need to get you to the hospital."

"I'm okay, Dad. I can paddle in." I try to protest, but seriously, lying down and closing my eyes sounds so good right now.

He grabs my ankle rope to pull my board over to us. "Millie, we're not taking a chance of you passing out again. Lie down. Now."

He drapes his arm over me as he starts swimming us in. A few other surfers walk over as we get to the shore.

"Is she okay?" one of them says as Dad picks me up in his arms.

"Yeah, she hit her head, but I think she's fine."

"Dad, I can walk," I say as I put my arm around his neck. Honestly, I'm not sure I can.

"Shh, Mills, just rest." He looks at the other surfers. "You mind grabbing our boards and bringing them to my truck?"

"Yeah, man. We've got you."

As Dad starts to walk to the truck, I put my head on his shoulder and close my eyes. "Dad, I got so dizzy before I wiped out, and I had motion sickness. I've never had that."

"Okay, sweetie. Let's go to the doctor and figure this out. You're fine." I can tell by the tone in his voice that he's starting to question if I am fine.

We're in the hospital room waiting for the doctor to get back with the results of some lab work she requested. She did some manual tests for a concussion but doesn't think I have one. She thinks I might have anemia.

"Dad, I feel a lot better," I say, looking up at him. He's still standing by the treatment table, holding my hand. "We've been waiting for like twenty minutes."

"We're not leaving," he says, squeezing my hand. "I don't care how long we have to wait—"

The doctor's smiling when she walks back in. I guess that's a good thing. "We have the results of your bloodwork. Maybe your dad would like to wait outside."

"What?" I say, frowning. "No, I want him here."

"Are you sure?" The doctor looks down at the lab results and then back up at me.

Dad's squeezing my hand so hard that I think he might break it. "Yes," I say. "Yes, of course, I'm sure."

"You're pregnant."

"What?" I say so quietly that I can barely hear myself.

Dad puts his arm around me to steady my slumping body.

"That's not possible. I'm on the pill."

"Did you miss any?" The doctor looks down at the results again like they're going to change. "Even if you didn't, the pill isn't perfect. You're pregnant. Have you had any other symptoms? Are you late?"

"Yeah, by like a week, but it happens sometimes when I'm stressed."

"And she's been dizzy," Dad says. "And getting an upset stomach."

The doctor nods her head. "All symptoms of pregnancy. Have you had any morning sickness?"

"I threw up my breakfast the other day, but I thought it was because the burrito was two days old."

The doctor laughs. "Yeah, it could have been that, but you're pregnant. Do you have an OB? I can recommend someone."

"We live in San Diego." When I say 'we,' I think of Mason. The panic must be all over my face.

The doctor pats my leg. "It's going to be fine. You're no more than a month pregnant. You don't have to see an OB right away. You can wait until you get back there, but in the meantime, stay off surfboards, okay? I'm giving you a supply of prenatal vitamins to start taking until you see your doctor. It's important to start taking them right away."

"I'll make sure she takes them," Dad says, pulling me closer to him.

The doctor nods. "You have a good Dad. Take some time in here if you need it. My nurse will bring the vitamins in. Good luck, Millie."

As she walks out, the tears start streaming down my face again. "Dad, I think I messed up?"

Dad sits down next to me. "Sweetie," he says as he takes my hands and squeezes them. "Mills, we're good. Everything's good. No matter what. Okay? Just tell me what's happening."

"When we were in Pakistan—after we found you and Mason got shot—I was so stressed out. I think I might have missed a few days of the pill. And Mason and I were together a few times in Pakistan."

He nods his head a few times and strokes his beard—like he always does when he's figuring something out. "Okay. It's all good. Everything's good. Are you ready to have a baby? Have you and Mason talked about it?"

"He's ready," I say. "He asked me to marry him a few months ago. And we talked about it again the other day. I wasn't ready when he asked me the first time, but I am now."

"You don't have to get married because you're pregnant—"

"No, Dad, this was before I knew I was pregnant. I love him. I want to marry him."

"Okay, that's between you and Mason, but the baby's separate from that. I'll support you no matter what you want to do, but you need to talk to Mason about it right away."

I look down. "He's looking for the guys who killed JJ. I don't want to distract him."

"Millie, you're telling him right now," he says, standing up. "If I have to dial the phone and tape it to your ear, you're telling him."

"Are you going to put me in a headlock?" I say, smiling at him.

"If I have to," he laughs. "Look, Mills, think about how different our lives would have been if Nejra's letter would have gotten to me. We would have been a family. I'd do anything to change what happened. No matter what was going on in my life back then, I would have wanted to know about you."

"He told me yesterday that Culver won't let him come back to California. He's going to be active in Virginia for another year."

Dad rubs his beard again. "We'll figure it out, but you need to tell him about the baby immediately."

"I don't expect him to quit even if I do tell him."

"He might not. I don't know, but you have to give him the option." He looks right in my eyes. "Mason's a different guy than I am. I don't think he's scared to quit at all. He knows what's waiting for him is better than what he has now, and he doesn't even know about the baby yet."

"What if he stays in and gets killed? What if he doesn't come home?"

Dad hugs me again. "Then you and I will raise the baby. And Chase and Mariel will help. We did a pretty great job raising you."

"Yeah, you did."

"One step at a time, Mills," he says as he kisses my forehead. "And just remember this: No matter what happens next, I'm here for you. No matter what you decide. No matter what you want to do. I'm here for you. I'm not leaving your side. You understand that?"

"Yeah," I say, smiling. "Thanks, Dad."

"Okay, let's get going. I'll drive you back to Virginia Beach so you can talk to Mason in person." He helps me off the table then holds me around the shoulders like he's trying to help me walk.

"Dad, I'm pregnant, not lame. I can walk." I roll my eyes and sigh loudly. "You're about to reach a whole new level of overprotective dad, aren't you?"

"I think you mean a whole new level of overprotective dad *and* grandpa," he says, smiling as he tightens his grip on my shoulders.

Chapter Thirty-Six

MASON, VIRGINIA BEACH, VIRGINIA, 2020

"Hey. I cleared Millie back." Butch looks at me like what he said should make sense. "She doesn't have her agency credentials anymore, so she's in the visitor's area."

"What? What are you talking about?"

"Millie. I'm talking about Millie. You remember her—blonde hair, sassy attitude."

I shake my head, hoping that it will jump-start my brain. "Millie's here? On the base?"

"Yeah. Like I just said. In the visitor's area. Were you not expecting her?"

"No. She's supposed to be in the Outer Banks. What's she doing here?"

"Do I know? I just cleared her back." He takes a few steps toward me and lowers his voice. "Are y'all having problems or something?"

"Not that I know of." I turn my head to the outside door. Suddenly I'm nervous.

"Maybe she's finally come to her senses and is here to break up with you."

I whip my head around and glare at him. "Shut up, Butch."

"I'm kidding, Mase. Damn. Don't kill the messenger." He steps back a few feet and points toward the door. "You know who would probably know why she's here? Millie. And as I mentioned several times, she's here, right now, two hundred yards from you."

He chuckles as he walks away. I'm not finding any of this funny. A million things are running through my mind right now and none of them are good. I open the door and see Millie sitting on a picnic table. An overwhelming feeling of déjà vu crashes into me. I feel like I've seen her sitting on that exact table before. I'm trying to get my brain to focus, but the memory feels far away.

As she looks over at me, I shake my head to try to get my mind back in the present. She waves and tries to smile. I can tell she's upset. I run over to her—covering the distance between us in a few seconds.

"Millie?" As I close in on her, I see her eyes are brimming with water. I can tell she's about to break down. I grab her by the shoulders. "What's wrong, baby?"

She rubs her eyes, causing a few tears to escape. "I'm fine. I just need to talk to you in person. I messed up, Mase."

I take a step back and inhale a long, slow breath. "Okay. Just tell me. Whatever it is. I don't care how bad it is. We're going to figure it out."

She looks up at me and nods. "Do you remember in Pakistan—the night you got out of the hospital—when we had sex?"

"Uh, yeah. I remember that very fondly," I say, laughing. "And if I remember correctly—and I think I do—you didn't mess up that night. In fact, you did a lot of things very right."

"Mase, no, I mean with everything happening there—finding dad, you getting shot. It was a lot," she says, wringing her hands. She looks down, "and I think I might have forgotten to take my pill for a few days."

I stop breathing for a second. "Wait. What?" I say, tilting her chin up as she bites her lip. "Are you pregnant?"

Before she can answer me, I lift her off the table and squeeze her to me. Her legs dangle back and forth in the air as she wraps her arms around my neck.

"I messed up," she whispers.

"You didn't mess up. Not at all. Not even a little bit."

I put her down and wipe the tears off her cheeks. She looks up at me and smiles a little.

"Do you know for sure?" I help her back onto the table. "Like how? I mean, not how. But, how do you know? Are you late?"

"Yeah, by a little more than a week. I'm rarely late. And I've been getting sick in the mornings. Remember when I threw up and you blamed the burrito? And Dad and I went surfing this morning. I got dizzy and fell off. I never fall off—"

"Mills," I say, pulling her against my chest. "That's really dangerous. Are you okay? Did you hit your head? You could have drowned."

"I'm fine. Dad was with me."

"Wait, does Mack know you might be pregnant?"

She looks up at me and squints her eyes—her lips lightly

pursed. "I was going to wait to tell you until you got the people who killed JJ, but Dad told me I had to tell you now. I don't want to distract you with what you have to do here."

I push my forehead into hers. "Are we ever going to get past you hiding stuff from me because you think you know better than I do what's best for me?"

"I'd like to say yes, but my record on this is really bad."

"Really bad. Like the worst," I say. "I guess I'm lucky to have Mack on my side."

"Yeah, he was not having any of my not telling you. He drove me here from the Outer Banks. He's still waiting for me in the parking lot. He's not letting me leave until I talk to you."

"He's a good man," I say. "How's he taking it?"

"He made us go right to the doctor after I fell off the board."

"Wait—"

"Oh, and Mase, one more thing, the doctor did a blood test. I'm pregnant."

I shake my head and hug her again. "I feel like you probably should have led with that."

"Yeah, I'm still trying to wrap my head around it," she says into my chest. "Mase, I'm pregnant."

I squeeze her tighter. "I'm here for you no matter what you decide. Seriously, no matter what."

"I want to have the baby," she says quietly.

I try not to let my voice mirror the joy that's suddenly surging through my body. "I thought you said you weren't ready to have a baby."

She sits back and looks up at me. "That was a long time ago."

"Mills," I say, smiling as I stroke her cheek. "That was a few months ago."

She leans her face into my hand. "I want this baby. I want your baby. I'm scared, but I want to have it."

"Baby, why are you scared? We're going to do this together—every step. I'm going to spoil you so much. Anything you want, it's yours."

She smiles, but her eyes are sad again. "I realize that you're here for a while. And I'm okay with it. Really. I'll be fine. Thousands of babies have been born with their fathers in service. I know you have to do what you have to do."

I guess she doesn't realize that there's no way in hell I'm letting her go through this alone. I smile and squeeze her hand. "Will you stay here for a second? There's something I need to do."

"What?" She looks at me—her brow furrowing. "What do you need to do?"

"Just stay here. I'll be right back."

As I charge through the door, I see Culver walking down the hall. I run after him and grab him by the shoulder, spinning him around.

"Did you know Millie was pregnant?"

"I did," he says, squaring up for what he obviously thinks is going to be a fight. "Mack called me."

"You chose Bravo over us to go wheels up today. Did you hold my team back because you knew she was coming here?"

He takes a step toward me and lowers his voice. "I did.

Professionally, it was absolutely the wrong decision, but I don't regret it one bit."

I grab him into an awkward hug. "Thank you, Harry. Thank you."

He lets me hug him for about three seconds before he pushes me back. He nods. "I told you when you came back that you were in or out. I won't send you back to Coronado, and I can't hold your team back again. I wanted to give Millie a chance to tell you in person, but that's all I can do. The only way out for you is a full retirement."

I take a deep breath. "I'm retiring. I'm officially retiring effective as soon as possible."

He locks his eyes with mine. "Mason, you only have another year for your twenty-year pension. Are you sure about this?"

"I've never been more sure of anything in my life."

He smiles and chucks me on the shoulder. "All right. You've never made a bad decision. I'll get the paperwork going. I'm happy for you."

When he turns around, I run to my locker, grab the box, and then run back outside to Millie. She's still looking at the door—waiting for me to come back out. Her eyes follow me as I walk over to her. I try to stop the grin that's covering my face, but there's just no way to hold it back.

"What?" she says, laughing. "What did you do?"

"I just officially retired."

"What?" Her eyes widen as her mouth drops open. "Like all the way? You only have a year left—"

I take her hands in mine. "And that's a year I'm going to

be spending with you and our baby. Final decision. I'm not missing out on a second of this."

"What about the people who killed JJ?"

"Mills, there are thousands of active SEALs—and thousands more in training—who are every bit as good as I am. They're going to find who killed JJ and take care of them." I look down at her stomach and gently run my hand over it. "But there's only one person who can be this baby's dad. I've been thinking there's not another job in the world that I would like as much as operating, but now I know I've found an even better one."

She smiles and puts her hand on top of mine.

"Can you feel anything?" I say as I spread my hand as wide as I can over her stomach.

"Nausea. A lot of nausea. I think our baby is trying to kill me."

I lean down and put my head in her lap. "Baby, it's your dad. Try to take it easy on your mom. She's amazing and she's going to be such a great mom to you. Just be cool. Maybe chill out a little bit for now."

Millie laughs as she rubs my head.

"Do you think he can hear me?" I say, pressing my ear against her stomach.

"I don't think he has ears yet, babe."

"I know he still heard me. We've got an agreement. He's going to take it easy on you."

She's shaking her head and smiling. Her face is glowing as I gently kiss her.

"I'm going to spoil this baby even more than Mack spoiled

you. I truly didn't think that was possible until this very moment."

"I know you will, babe. You're going to be a great dad."

I hug her one more time before I stand up and then drop down on my knee. "There's just one more thing we have to take care of—"

She nods as her eyes start filling up again.

"Millie, I've known from the first second I saw you that I wanted to spend the rest of my life with you." I take her hand as I pull the ring box out of my pocket. "Will you please marry me?"

She nods her head vigorously—the tears streaming down her face.

"Use your words, please," I say, smiling as I stand up and put the ring on her finger.

"Yes," she says, her voice shaking. "Yes. I'll marry you. I love you so much."

"I love you, baby," I whisper into her ear. "Let's get out of here, so I can start taking proper care of my fiancé and my baby."

I help her off the table and sweep her up into my arms.

She laughs. "Why does everyone think I can't walk all of a sudden? Mase, pregnant women can walk."

"Not on my watch, you can't," I say, kissing the top of her head. "Your feet aren't going to touch the ground for nine months and maybe not even after that."

Epilogue

MILLIE, SAN DIEGO, CALIFORNIA, 2021

"Oh my God. I just saw you a week ago." Chase's eyes widen as he opens his arms for a hug. "You're so much bigger."

I try to position my enormous baby bump against him for a hug. "That's not what pregnant women like to hear. Just FYI."

He laughs as he releases me. "I know I don't have to tell you how beautiful you look. You're glowing. But it does look like you're going to deliver in about ten minutes? When's he due again?"

"About three weeks, but it can't come soon enough. He's kicked me for about two months straight," I say, sighing. He pulls out my chair and helps lower my huge body into it. "Thanks for meeting me for lunch. I had to get out of the house. Dad and Mason are putting the last touches on the nursery. The paint smell was too much."

"I'm happy you called me," he says, taking the seat opposite me. "Mar's still up in L.A. with her sister, but she said to tell you hi."

"I wanted to talk to both of you, but you can relay the message." I reach out and take his hand. "I talked to Mason. We want you and Mar to be the baby's godparents."

His eyes start to fill up as he walks around the table and pulls me to him for another hug. "Yes. Absolutely yes. We would be honored although I'm not sure if we're worthy of it."

"Chase, you were already my maid of honor at our wedding. Who else do you think I'm going to choose to be my baby's godfather?"

"I thought maybe Mack would be his godfather."

"He's the grandpa. If anything happens to us, he takes over, but he's going to need your help, just like he did for raising me."

He smiles, a few tears rolling down his cheek. "Nothing's going to happen to you. This baby is going to have six people around him at all times. I think he's going to be even more spoiled than you."

"Funny." I'm about to smack him when I feel something pop in my body. All of a sudden, a gush of water spills out onto my chair. I sit up straight and breathe in quickly.

"What?" Chase grabs my arm. "Millie, what? What's wrong?"

I look over at him and exhale slowly. "I think my water just broke."

He looks under my chair. "Yep, looks like it might have," he says in a very soothing tone.

"It's too early, Chase," I say, my voice shaking. "He's not due yet."

"Well, babies have a funny way of setting their own timetables." He looks up and sees my wide eyes. "Millie, he'll be fine. He's plenty big enough to be born. He's just impatient like his grandpa and his dad and his godfather. He has no choice, but to come early."

I nod, but I'm finding it hard to speak.

Chase helps me up carefully. "Come on. We need to go to the hospital. Have you been having contractions this morning?"

"I've had the Braxton Hicks stuff for a month or so, but—" I look up at him. "They've been a lot worse this morning. Oh my God. I think I'm in labor."

"I think you are." He smiles and hugs me again. "We've got this. No need to worry. Let's get in my car. I'll take you to the hospital. All you need to do is call your doctor and call Mason. I'll do the rest."

When he gets in the car, I'm staring at my phone.

"You can do it, sweetie. Doctor first," he says, pointing to the phone. "Do you want me to call for you?"

I shake my head as I push the number for my doctor. "Hi, this is Millie Marsh, I mean Davis. This is Millie Davis. I think I'm in labor."

Epilogue

Mack and I are popping open some beers and admiring our handiwork on the nursery when my phone rings.

"It's Millie. They probably want us to come up and join them." I put the phone on speaker. "Hey, babe. We just finished the nursery. It's all ready for him."

"Uh," she says slowly, "that's a good thing because I think he's coming today."

Mack and I look at each other and then down at the phone. "What? Babe, what's happening? Are you okay?" I say, taking the phone off speaker and putting it to my ear.

"I think I'm in labor." Her voice is a little shaky. "My water broke."

"Okay, it's go time. Where are you? I'm coming to get you." I walk quickly to our closet, grab her already-packed overnight bag, and throw it on the bed.

"Chase is with me. He's taking me to the hospital. Just meet us there. Okay?" Her voice breaks a few times.

"You're fine, babe. Mack and I are leaving right now. Chase will take care of you until we get there. Okay? I love you so much."

"I love you, Mason. Hurry, okay?"

I hear the phone click and turn around. Mack's a foot from me. His face looks like he's about ready to go into battle. "She's in labor?"

"Yeah, I think so. Her water broke. Chase is taking her to the hospital." I'm just standing there staring at him. I think I'm a little in shock.

Mack grabs Millie's bag off the bed. "Let's go, Dad. I'm driving."

When we get to the hospital, Mack and I run down the hall to her room. When we get there, a nurse is taking Millie's blood pressure. I run around the other side of her bed.

"Baby," I say, taking her face into my hands. "Are you okay?"

She nods as the nurse looks at us. "Well look at this," the nurse says, laughing. "You've substituted the first man for two more. Are either of these the dad?"

"This one's the baby daddy," Millie says, patting my chest. She reaches for Mack's hand as he walks to the bed. "And this one's my dad. Can they both stay?"

"Neither one of them can stay if they don't get out of this room and put some scrubs on." She looks at us scornfully. "Your clothes look like a paint can exploded on them. Cover all that up right now."

"Yes, ma'am," I say, kissing Millie one more time. "We're on it."

We rush out of the room and to the nurses' station. They move much too slowly to get us our scrubs. When we get them on, we run back to the room as Chase is returning from parking our cars. The three of us burst into the room.

The nurse grabs her chest. "Good Lord, you almost gave me a heart attack."

"Sorry," I say as I try to slowly walk over to Millie. "I didn't want to miss anything."

"Well, she didn't give birth in the two minutes since you've been gone. I swear first-time fathers give me a headache."

She laughs as she looks back at Millie. "Child, you have men coming out of the woodwork. Where's your momma? Or maybe a sister?"

"Only child and my mom died right after I was born." Mack grabs her hand and squeezes it.

"Oh, baby. I'm so sorry," the nurse says. "I'll take care of you."

"Thanks, Ruby," Millie says, smiling. "Does everything look okay?"

"Absolutely. All your vital signs are good," Ruby says. "The doctor said the baby's going to be here soon. You're ready for an epidural if you still want one."

Millie groans and grabs her stomach. "Ahh!" She closes her eyes. "Yes, please. I want all the medicine."

"What's happening?" I look up at Ruby as Millie squeezes my hand tighter.

Ruby rolls her eyes. "She's having a contraction. Settle down. Get her through this one and I'll get the anesthesiologist."

"Millie," I whisper as I put my head against hers. "You're doing so great. Squeeze my hand harder. Break it if you have to. That's right. Squeeze Mack's hand, too."

Chase walks over to a screen that looks like it's charting heart rates. "This is the line that shows contractions," he says calmly. It's clear he's done this before. "Here she is right now. Mills, this one is almost over."

Millie opens her eyes and nods her head. "Where's Ruby?" she whispers. "I want the epidural."

Mack lets go of her hand. "I'll go look for her."

Chase kisses Millie's forehead. "You'll be fine. I'm going to the waiting room to call Mar. I'll call Butch, too, and Carol. Everyone will be thinking about you, okay? I'll be back after the little guy arrives. I can't wait to meet him."

As he walks through the door, I look down at Millie. "Are you okay, baby?"

"My back hurts so much, Mase," she whimpers. "I just want him to be here."

I've never felt this helpless. I put my face against hers. "Baby, he's going to be here soon. You're doing so great. Just a little bit longer, okay? I love you so much. You're the strongest person I know."

"Okay, Millie," Ruby says as she walks back in with Mack following closely behind her. "We're here. The pain will go away pretty soon. Just a little pinch and you'll feel so much better."

They roll her over and insert a needle into her back. When she winces, I almost cry out. Ruby looks up at me and nods to the guy with the needle. "From the look on the dad's face, he's going to need an epidural, too."

Epilogue

The baby's on my chest when Dad walks back into the room. During the delivery, he stepped into the hallway to give us privacy. I asked Mason to tell him to come back in.

"Dad, this is your grandson, Mo," I say, kissing the baby's head.

"Mo Davis. I like it. That's a tough name," Dad says, smiling as he touches Mo's back gently.

"That's his nickname. That's what we're going to call him, but his real name is Mack Joseph after you and Mason's grandpa."

Dad takes a quick breath, his eyes starting to fill up. "You named him after me?"

"Of course. I can't think of a better role model for him." I reach out to take Dad's hand.

"And you're okay with that?" Dad says, looking up at Mason.

"Can't think of a better name for him," Mason says, smiling as he picks Mo up. "You want to hold him, Grandpa?"

"So much." Dad takes Mo in his big arms and starts rocking him slowly. "Hey, little guy, I'm your grandpa. We have the same name. Everyone will call you Mo, but I think I'll call you Mack Two. Does that sound okay to you? It does? Okay, it's settled. I'm Mack One and you're Mack Two. We're going to be best friends."

Mason crawls into bed with me. "I don't think we're ever going to get him back," he whispers as he puts his arm around me.

"Where are Dad and Chase?" I say as I slowly swing my legs over the hospital bed.

It's discharge day. I'm a little scared about doing this without Ruby's help, but Mariel and Carol got back in town yesterday, so I have backup.

"They went down to the car to check that I've installed the baby seat correctly?" Mason laughs.

"Oh my God," I say, shaking my head. "That's so obnoxious. I'm sorry."

"No, it's cool. I don't mind having my work checked where you and Mo are concerned." He leans over and kisses me. "Except in one area, of course."

I slide my hands under his T-shirt and start exploring his chest. "I feel like it's been forever since we've had sex. I'm getting impatient."

"Just a few more weeks, baby," he says, kissing my neck.

"Oh for glory's sake, she just had a baby. Can you hold off on impregnating her again for maybe like a day or two?" Ruby storms into the room, holding an enormous vase of white roses. "And maybe quit sending her flowers. You're making all the other mothers jealous."

"Hi, Ruby. I missed you," Mason says, smiling. "And those flowers are not from me."

She rolls her eyes at Mason and turns to me. "Okay, missy, which of your other two men are they from?"

"I seriously don't know. Dad and Chase know I'm leaving today. I don't think they would have sent more flowers."

"So now you have a fourth man coming at you?" she says. "Now the nurse is getting jealous. You need to pass at least one of them off to me."

"I'm right here, Ruby. Take me." Mason reaches his hands out to her.

"Boy, please," she says, swatting his hands as she comes over to me. "You can't handle this little ray of sunshine. There's no way you could handle me. And you know I've got my eyes on Mack. He's got a dangerous look underneath all that quiet that makes me want to—Oh Lord, Millie, you've got to leave this hospital and take all your men with you."

"We're leaving in a few minutes," I say as she hugs me. "I'm going to miss you."

"Honey, I know you will." She takes one more peek at Mo —who's fast asleep—and leaves the room as quickly as she came in.

"You think we should tell her Carol's moving in with Dad?"

"Hell no," Mason says. "I want to leave this hospital in one piece."

Mason walks over to the flowers and grabs the attached card. "You want me to read it or do you have a secret lover?"

"You already know Butch is my secret lover," I say. "They're probably from him."

He laughs and opens the card. He scans it, sighs deeply, and hands the card to me.

Congratulations on your new addition.
When you get tired of playing house, the offer still stands.
Paul Ward

"Good God, he does not give up," I say, throwing the card on the bed. "He has to know we're not interested by now, right?"

"Mmm," Mason says, pursing his lips.

"What? You're interested now?"

He sits next to me on the bed. "I mean not right now, but we have to earn a living at some point."

"I don't think that's the way, especially with a baby."

"We don't have to be in on the dangerous stuff. We'll have Butch and Hawk for that." He rubs his beard and looks down at me. "Private jets, luxury villas, two-day missions. There are worse ways to earn money."

I squint my eyes. "Hmm. I can't even focus on it right now. Let's give it a year and then maybe consider coming back—if they still want us."

"Oh, they'll still want us."

We both look over as Mo starts crying.

"I think Mo's ready to go home," I say, smiling as Mason picks him up. "Are you ready?"

He hands him to me and helps me down into the wheel-chair. "Yeah, baby, let's go home," he whispers as he kisses the top of my head. "Let's go home."

Epilogue

RAINE

The Trident Trilogy crew is back in my novel, *Raine Out.*

The first chapter of Raine Out.
Nine Months Later
Raine

"Did you get one or two beds in our room?" Butch says as he walks across the patio, stuffing the last of a cheeseburger into his mouth.

"We have separate rooms." I cross my arms firmly over my chest. "You already know that."

"Are you going to give me a key to your room? Or do I have to breach the door?"

Hawk wanders over from where he's manning the barbecue grill. "Butch, depending on the hotel, I think you can probably bust it with a battering ram. I don't think you'll need to bring explosives."

As of today, Butch and Hawk are officially former Navy SEALs. We're at their retirement party. But even in civilian life, I have no doubt they'll use their skills—including kicking in any door that's inconveniencing them.

"Stop it!" I say, reaching up to shove them in their chests. "He's only coming with me as cover—so my friends won't try to set me up."

I'm barely five foot, four. These guys tower over me, but I learned quickly when I started working with them that they respond much faster to physical feedback.

Hawk looks down at me and shakes his head. "Shoving isn't effective, Raine. I've told you before to go for the balls if you want to immobilize a man—"

"No! Don't say a word." I point at Butch as he swallows his comeback—his face almost bursting as he tries to control his grin.

I've worked with these guys for almost five years as the CIA liaison to the SEAL teams in Virginia Beach. They're like big brothers to me. They're no more interested in dating me than I am in dating them. When I asked Butch to be my plus-one to a friend's wedding, I knew I'd have to endure hours of teasing, but I had no idea it would be this relentless.

"You know," Butch says, pulling a piece of food out of his beard, "you told me you were a lesbian the first day I met you. Maybe tell your friends that."

"I told you that because you very inappropriately asked me to get a drink with you ten seconds after we met." I slap his hand as he puts the leftover crumb of food in his mouth. "Gross. Don't eat food out of your beard. And telling my friends I'm a lesbian won't stop them. They'll just try to set me up with a woman."

"God, I'd be so in favor of that," he says, closing his eyes and letting out a long breath.

I shove him again. "Stop thinking about me with a woman."

"Never. And so we're clear, I asked you to get a drink because you were so quiet. I was trying to help you fit into the team—not trying to sleep with you."

"Are you sure you weren't trying to do both?" I say, crossing my arms over my chest again.

"I guess we'll find out on St. John." He grabs my arm as I try to backhand him and curls up my hand. "Slapping doesn't work as a self-defense move. Ball up that fist to get the most impact. Ask Millie. She knows."

He nods to something over my shoulder. I turn around to see Millie—my best friend since our agency training days—standing a foot away from us. I grab her arm and pull her over. "Will you please tell him to stop torturing me? You're the only one he listens to—"

"Since when does Butch listen to me?" Millie tries to pinch his cheek. He spins her around and puts her in a fake chokehold. This is the way SEALs play. We're used to it.

"Hey! Easy," Millie's husband, Mason, swoops in and pulls her away from Butch. He wraps her protectively in his arms. "She just had a baby."

"You can't tell me what to do. I don't work for you anymore," Butch says, laughing.

Mason was the leader of the SEAL team until he retired about a year ago to be with Millie and their new baby.

"No," Millie says, raising her eyebrows, "now you work for me. I'm going to be a much tougher boss than Mason ever was."

Millie resigned from the CIA, but the director convinced her to run a special projects division out of San Diego—where she and Mason live. I'm on a month's hiatus as I transfer out there to be her agency handler.

"Will you tell me how you're going to discipline me, Mills?" Butch rubs his hands together. "Be as specific as you can. The good stuff's in the details."

Mason whacks Butch on the side of the head and looks at me. "Are you sure you want to take this Neanderthal with you to your friend's wedding?"

"I don't want to take him at all, but the rest of the team are active—except Hawk—and he wouldn't be any better," I whine. "Mills, will you please let Mason have a hall pass for the weekend? I'd much rather take him."

"Why do you have to take anyone?" Millie says as Mason pulls her tighter against him and kisses the top of her head. They're the sweetest couple I've ever known. When I'm around them, I can't help thinking I'm never going to find anything close to what they have.

"You know how my childhood friends are. They're different than us," I say, sighing. "I don't want to spend the entire weekend answering questions about my dating status and/or my sexual orientation. I shouldn't even go. I'm canceling."

"Excuse us," Millie says to the guys as she takes my arm and pulls me across the patio. She grabs my shoulders and gets in my face. "You're going. It will do you good. When's the last time you've had more than a day off? It's only for a long weekend. You know Butch will be a blast. He's just teasing you."

"I know," I say, covering my face. "It's not about him. I haven't been around my old friends for so long. It's not the same anymore. You know how it is when you hang out with people who aren't in the business. I can't even tell them what I do for a living. What do you tell your childhood friends?"

"I don't have any childhood friends. When I left home, I cut all ties. You know that." She takes a step back. "And it wasn't healthy. You've kept in touch with Sophie—"

"She kept in touch with me. No matter how much I ignore her, she keeps coming back."

"Good." Millie wraps me into a hug. "Sophie's cool. I liked her when she spent the weekend with us in D.C."

"She liked you, too. Maybe you should come with me instead of Butch."

"Are you forgetting I have a baby who's literally almost always attached to me?" She squeezes me again before she releases me from the hug. "And if you took me, they would definitely think we're a couple. Didn't Sophie already ask you that?"

"Yeah, I think she roots for us to be a couple."

"She ain't the only one," Butch says as he walks up behind us.

"Are you still trying to live out that fantasy?" Millie slugs his shoulder. "We've told you if we ever hook up, you'll be the first to know."

"And I await that news anxiously," he says as he puts his arm around me. "You know I'm just messing with you. I'll behave like the perfect gentleman when we get there. And I'm the best wingman ever created if you require those services."

"Are you really taking this idiot with you?" Millie's dad, Mack, walks over holding her adorable son, Mo.

"You know I'd take you if Carol would let me." I smile a little too broadly. I've had a crush on Mack from the second I met him. He's a retired SEAL, too. But unlike all of these other guys, I find him wildly attractive. He's almost dangerously tough, but it's his boundless tender side that makes my heart ache. "You're everyone's first choice, Mack."

"He's definitely mine," Butch says, taking a step away from Mack in case he swings at him. It wouldn't be the first time.

Mack shakes his head at Butch. "You better treat this young woman like the queen she is. If I hear you didn't, I'll kick your ass and enjoy every second of it."

"Yes, sir," Butch says, saluting him. "I think you're the only person who could kick my ass, but only because you fight dirty—"

"Damn straight I do," Mack snarls, "especially when I'm protecting my daughters."

Mack's started calling me his daughter. It's adorable and it's made me crush on him even harder. I know he's not an option. It's the only thing that keeps me from acting like a complete idiot in front of him. As soon as a hot guy starts showing me any attention, I become totally awkward. I've been that way since I was a teenager.

"Whatever you say, chief," Butch says as he walks away. "You know I don't want any part of you."

Mo starts crying and reaching for Millie.

"Mills, he's hungry again," Mack says, handing him to her. "I've already fed him the two bottles you packed in the cooler, so we're going to have to go directly to the source. I swear he eats as much as I do."

Millie starts to reach into her sundress to pull out a breast for Mo.

"No!" I put my hands up to stop her. "Millie! No!"

"Raine, it's just a boob," she says as Mason leaps across a lawn chair and starts pushing her toward the house.

"I know it's natural and nothing's wrong with it," he says as Millie tries to resist, "but there's not a chance in hell you're breastfeeding him in front of these deviants. Hawk said you could use his bedroom."

"Fine. Come with me, Raine." Millie grabs my hand as she kisses the strawberry blond curls starting to form on Mo's head. "We're not finished with this discussion."

I follow her back to the bedroom—head down and dragging my feet—like a kid who's about to be disciplined.

"Raine Nira Laghari," she says, patting the spot next to her on the bed. "Do you want to tell me what's really going on? Why are you resisting this trip so much?"

"Damn, using my full name." I plop down on the bed. "You sound like my mom."

"I love your mom. That's a compliment."

"God, she loves you, too. I shouldn't have brought you home for Christmas that first year we met."

"Did I tell you she sent Mo a Baby Ganesh? It's enormous. It almost takes up half of his room."

I groan. "Ugh, Millie, why did you have a baby? She won't stop talking about him. She legitimately thinks she's his grandma. She keeps texting me that picture you sent her—like I haven't seen him already. She thinks it will encourage me to get married and start popping out kids."

"Ding, ding, ding. We have a winner." Millie smiles. "Finally, we're getting to the real reason you don't want to go on this trip."

———

Buy or download Raine Out on Amazon.

What's Next?

The Trident Trilogy crew's story continues in the second and third books of The Grand Slam Series, *Raine Out* and *Leave It On The Field*, and in the second and third books of The Blitzen Bay Series, *No One Wants That* and *Pretty Close To Perfect*.

Truth or Tequila is the first book of The Grand Slam Series.

The Runaway Bride of Blitzen Bay is the first book of The Blitzen Bay Series.

Go to donnaschwartze.com for a suggested reading order. While you're there, sign up for my email newsletter to be the first to know when I publish new books.

All of my books are available on Amazon.

About the Author

Donna Schwartze is a graduate of the University of Missouri School of Journalism. She also holds a Master of Arts from Webster University. She is an avid yogi and plans to still be able to do the splits on her 100th birthday. Her favorite character from her books is Mack from The Trident Trilogy.